"If there's a curse, Dex, I'll help you find it."

Lara made the promise easily, knowing that this was an appropriate use of her talents. Dexter turned toward her then. Laying his hand on her arm, he spoke quietly. Emphatically.

But she had no idea what he was saying. His touch caused a psychic shock of outrageous proportions.

"Please." Lara couldn't handle the images of his past that mingled with the strain of her attraction to him. Her breath came in shallow gulps and she realized her heart was pounding twice as fast as normal.

He looked confused and...aroused?

"What do you see?" His voice scratched along her senses, teasing her with a hungry quality that robbed her of reason.

"It's never happened to me before, but I can see all your sexual thoughts."

Blaze™

Dear Reader,

I've always been fascinated by the idea of luck. In our world of mathematical statistics and calculated probabilities, it seems as if the whole concept of luck would be an antiquated notion, yet we talk about it all the time. We want the luck of the Irish or the horoscope with the most lucky stars. We wish good luck upon friends going off to an interview or new venture. My character Dexter Brantley would be quick to remind you that even the outcomes of NFL games can be determined by luck when possession of the football in overtime is dictated by a coin flip.

So what if a person loses their luck? Is there any way to retrieve it? These are the questions Dex faces when Lady Luck takes him for a ride. I hope you'll enjoy his story, which takes place in the gorgeous Thousand Island region between the U.S. and Canada. I've long wanted to set a book here, and Dex's privileged background gave me the perfect opportunity.

Happy reading,

Joanne Rock

JOANNE ROCK
Getting Lucky

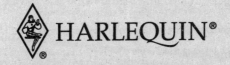

HARLEQUIN®

TORONTO • NEW YORK • LONDON
AMSTERDAM • PARIS • SYDNEY • HAMBURG
STOCKHOLM • ATHENS • TOKYO • MILAN • MADRID
PRAGUE • WARSAW • BUDAPEST • AUCKLAND

ISBN-13: 978-0-373-79385-3
ISBN-10:   0-373-79385-5

GETTING LUCKY

ABOUT THE AUTHOR

From *To Catch a Thief* to *Body Heat* and *The Big Easy*, RITA® Award-nominated author Joanne Rock loves a sexy suspense story where the hero and heroine aren't quite sure how far to trust one another. Joanne's thirst for writing a wide range of stories has revisited this theme in modern and medieval tales alike. Her books have been reprinted in twenty-two countries and translated into sixteen languages. A former college teacher and public relations coordinator, she has a master's degree in English from the University of Louisville and started writing when she became a stay-at-home mom. Learn more about Joanne and her work by visiting her at www.joannerock.com.

Books by Joanne Rock

HARLEQUIN BLAZE
108—GIRL'S GUIDE TO
    HUNTING & KISSING*
135—GIRL GONE WILD*
139—DATE WITH A DIVA*
171—SILK CONFESSIONS†
182—HIS WICKED WAYS†
240—UP ALL NIGHT
256—HIDDEN OBSESSION**
305—DON'T LOOK BACK††
311—JUST ONE LOOK††
363—A BLAZING LITTLE
    CHRISTMAS
    "His for the Holidays"

*Single in South Beach
†West Side Confidential
**Perfect Timing
††Night Eyes

HARLEQUIN SIGNATURE SELECT SPOTLIGHT
THE PLEASURE TRIP

HARLEQUIN ANTHOLOGY
BET ME
    "The Wildcard"

HARLEQUIN HISTORICAL
749—THE BETROTHAL
    "Highland Handfast"
758—MY LADY'S FAVOR
769—THE LAIRD'S LADY
812—THE KNIGHT'S COURTSHIP
890—A KNIGHT MOST WICKED

1

TWELVE YEARS of representing some of the nation's top athletic talent had earned Dexter Brantley a reputation as a lucky bastard. The epithet was sometimes shouted in anger as in the time when a lucrative endorsement deal with a new shoe company—founded by a former college roommate—earned him and his clients tens of millions. Sometimes the moniker was spoken in dazed wonder, as in the time a snooty skating star had been reluctant to sign with him for fear of sacrificing her precious art for the sake of fat professional contracts—until she'd seen exactly *how much* money Dexter could flood into her bank account.

After one of the most successful rises to the top of sports agenting imaginable, Dexter didn't mind the nickname no matter how it was used. In fact right now, as he sat in a nine-car pileup on the George Washington Bridge during the morning rush hour with a hundred cars honking behind him, he decided he'd give anything to feel like a lucky bastard again.

His cell phone rang as an emergency vehicle threaded through the pandemonium behind him, blocking out the shouts of the pissed-off Turkish cabdriver waving his fist just outside Dexter's smashed-up new Escalade.

Ignoring the cabbie and the steaming wreckage of a bread delivery truck silhouetted behind him, Dex answered the call and spoke into the headset that never left his ear while he was in the car.

"Brantley. What do you have for me?"

"I have a fairly angry catcher and his utterly livid new wife in your office who expected to meet you five minutes ago to discuss his free agency when—"

"Trish, I'm going to need you to handle this one for me." Dex fought the urge to jump into the brawl the cabbie so obviously wanted now that the guy's sweaty nose was pressed to the window right beside Dex's ear while he screamed at him. "There's a huge mess on the George Washington. A tractor trailer rear-ended a bread truck that slid into a whole slew of other—"

"No, Dex." Trish's voice was totally unsympathetic. "You'd better be on that elevator on your way up here now because Mark Setano's wife is totally losing it in the waiting room. I think she just tore your autographed Bucky Dent jersey off the wall."

Through the growing fog of condensation on the driver's side window, Dexter heard a banging on the car and decided he was ready to give the cabbie the fight he wanted.

"If she hurts that jersey, I'm suing," Dex growled to Trish before he tore off the headset and forcefully threw open the car door.

Right into a cop who had apparently come over to ask about the accident.

The officer doubled over for only a moment before he half straightened with a snarl on his red face.

"Oh God." Dex reached to steady the guy or extend an apology—damn, he didn't know what to do.

"It's his fault," the cabbie chimed in, pointing to Dex as he spoke in silky smooth English. "He was driving too fast, zipping in and out of the traffic on the bridge."

"Wait—" Dex could see the inauspicious tenor of this conversation and realized his day was going to hell even faster on this end than it was in his Manhattan office right now.

The officer straightened fully, his injuries apparently not keeping him from reaching for the pink and yellow pad of tickets inside his jacket. Swiping away a small spot of blood from his nose, the cop looked meaningfully at Dex and then back at the cabbie as he clicked open his pen to get started.

"So what did he do?"

Dex slumped back against his car door, unwilling to open his mouth again since he had a way of making more trouble than he cleared up lately. Ever since he'd turned thirty-three and the rumors of the Brantley family curse had surfaced out of ancient history to bite him squarely in the ass.

Several of his biggest-earning athletes had experienced a freakish run of bad luck and when a national newswire picked up some hometown history article about the misfortunes of a bunch of his dead relatives, others left his agency. Then a chimney fire burned his Aspen home to the ground a week before his Manhattan apartment had an electrical fire.

Looking around at the traffic pileup behind the twisted hoods of wrecked cars and slow-moving emergency vehicles, Dex knew he couldn't avoid taking action to curb the downward spiral of the last six months. No one was calling him a lucky bastard anymore, and he hadn't realized until just this minute how much of his business had been built on that image.

He needed his luck back. And right after the cop finished writing the third—no, make that the fourth—ticket, Dexter would swallow some pride and risk his libido to make the only phone call he could think of that might help the situation.

"CAN YOU GET THAT?" Lara Wyland kicked aside an empty paint tray and pulled out a crate of old case files as she called to her assistant.

In the two weeks since her move to new office space outside of Albany, New York, she hadn't managed to get much work done. The historic carriage house still smelled like the paint she'd slapped on the walls herself, the fumes aggravating her psychic senses even more than her nose.

Where was her folder full of her credentials? She needed the extra ammunition for a fiery letter she planned to send to an online community of psychics who'd recently launched a smear campaign against her business. The old biddies were her mother's friends, certain they knew the best way to do everything while the new generation of psychics—like Lara—didn't know anything.

"Get what?" Jamie asked a moment later, sticking his head into her Moroccan-style office while juggling a coffee mug that read GhostFest 2007 and a stack of books from his morning class at the community college. At twenty-two, Jamie had gotten a late start on college after spending a few years in business for himself as a computer tech, but at least he knew what he wanted in life and hadn't let a delay in his chosen career path slow him down the way Lara had.

The phone rang almost as soon as he asked the question and he rolled his eyes in response.

"I hate it when you do that," he shouted to her as he jogged down the hallway painted in Tuscan Sunset to retrieve the cordless phone on his desk.

"Sorry," Lara called after him. Her brain had been back-firing with too much psychic energy from the lack of use in the past few weeks. Lately she shut down her computer just by touching it and her digital clock went back to 12:00 a.m. if she got within a three-foot radius. "I thought it had already rung once."

She couldn't help that she anticipated events. Although she usually only saw small things with her precognition—like a phone about to ring—rather than big, life-altering moments such as the murder of a friend's father in high school, Lara rarely sensed an event until it was just about to happen. So her moments of psychic forecasting were generally useless, unlike her deeper retrocognition gifts that had helped her build a thriving career in psychic investigations and—when the situation arose—the occasional foray into ghost hunting.

The work was challenging and often meaningful when she helped locate missing persons or important evidence. Remembering as much prevented her from being too touchy when other psychics accused her of using her gifts like a carnival sideshow, as a recent letter to the editor of a well-known psi magazine suggested.

Her sideline work as a ghost hunter might seem a bit

fluffy to people who hoped to refine the reputation of the psi community, but damn it, that kind of work provided the cash flow to her pro bono jobs for clients with missing kids.

And bottom line, her gifts were of the "use it or lose it" variety. She needed to exercise her talents or they started backfiring in strange ways, the unused energy messing with her personal electromagnetic field until she shorted out every clock, cell phone and laptop within a hundred yards. Witness the psychomagnetic explosions in her office this week.

"Lara?" Jamie shouted to her from the other room, their new intercom system not hooked up yet and probably not necessary since Lara usually knew when to pick up the phone anyhow. Apparently, she was off her game today.

Damn paint fumes.

"Yeah?"

"There's a guy on the phone who would like to speak with you but declined to tell me why. A Mr. Dexter Brantley."

Lara wished she didn't remember that name, but five years after her one-and-only meeting with the almighty sports agent to the stars, Dexter Brantley, she hadn't forgotten. The man was lethally handsome, rolling in dough—and completely dismissive of her work. Why would he ever call her when he had zero respect for her and her job?

"The sports agent?" She stalled, setting aside her folders to brace herself for whatever the hotshot New Yorker might want with her.

"He didn't reveal that, either," Jamie called, his voice getting closer as he stalked back down the hall to personally deliver the handset along with the book of fabric swatches she'd left in his office earlier during a debate about pillow coverings. He pressed the phone into her hand before spinning on his heel. "I thought maybe this was a personal matter."

He turned to grin at her over his shoulder before shutting the door behind him—something he hadn't done in all the weeks they'd been conducting business while settling into the new space. But then, Jamie was a closet romantic convinced Lara needed a man in her life. No doubt he was only trying to help.

In his defense, Jamie had no idea what kind of man lurked on the other end of the phone. A memory of steel-gray eyes and a chiseled jaw flashed through her mind and as she held the phone with him on it, she thought she caught a glimpse of him in real time, pacing a floor somewhere with his tie undone, waiting impatiently for her to pick up.

Lara stared down at the cordless handset and finally turned off the hold button.

"This is Lara Wyland." She sent out a frosty vibe, unwilling to take any snide jokes from this man and his high-powered ego. Heart-melting good looks didn't win a guy any points in her book if he was judgmental on the inside.

"This is Dexter Brantley." He launched into conversation without bothering to greet her. "You may not remember me—"

"I remember you."

She twirled an antique globe perched on her desk and had a vivid memory of this man laughing his Armani-covered ass off over her intention to remove a curse from a struggling NFL kicker's leg. Brantley had been the guy's agent at the time and he'd displayed great amusement at the player's belief that his Santeria-practicing grandmother had put a curse on Victor's kicking leg when her grandson had forgotten her birthday. She'd often wondered if the almighty Brantley had noticed Victor split the uprights his next thirty field goal attempts, before he'd fallen into a drug habit that had bankrupted him and prematurely ended his career, according to her local sports page.

"I won't waste your time, Ms. Wyland. I'm calling to find out if you're still in the business of removing curses."

"Call me Lara. And my work is far more wide-ranging than removing curses for people who actually *believe* in them." She couldn't deny the extra emphasis she put on the last bit, frustrated by the recent spurt of psychic-bashing in her life lately. "But I am open to such cases."

She'd accomplished too much in her decade-long career to subject herself to the scorn of disbelievers or the back-stabbing of holier-than-thou colleagues who didn't like the way she ran her business. But then, she and her mom had never seen eye to eye. It came as no surprise now that her mother would enlist her friends to publicly wage a battle she and Lara had carried on in private for years.

"I see." He paused briefly. "You're suggesting you won't work for people who don't buy into the idea of curses?"

"There isn't really a point then, Mr. Brantley, since a curse doesn't exist if the unfortunate individual doesn't recognize his problems as such." Shoving the globe aside she went to work organizing some aromatherapy oils in a glass case beside her desk, unwilling to give Brantley her full attention.

She'd moved into a more public office space to provide quality, beneficial psychic services to the masses and that's just what she was going to do. But damn it, she could draw the line at helping any friend of a man who thought her work was a hysterical waste of time, couldn't she?

"Call me Dex. And what if the unfortunate party simply wants to cover all his bases by investigating the curse angle in addition to some other reasons for all the bad luck?"

Lara opened a bottle of lavender oil and sniffed it in the hope of inhaling some relaxation.

"In that case, I would suggest all other avenues are explored first since, as some people are quick to point out, psychic services can be as efficient as the liberal use of snake oil on a problem." She recalled his assessment of her talent perfectly. And, to her mind, Dex's quick dismissal of her skills had been in large part to blame when her curse removal efforts had taken much longer than they should have.

Victor Marek had believed his leg cursed and thought Lara's help could "cure" him. And they probably would have taken care of the issue in about ten minutes of focused thinking and discussion if Lara had been left to simply do her job. But the slick sports agent's ridicule had made Victor doubt her, himself and the truth of his grandma's curse in the first place. And Lara's confidence hadn't been helped by Brantley's sudden switch from flirting with her to— when he discovered why she was there—laughing at her. They hadn't made real headway with Victor's problem until hours later when she'd finally ushered Brantley out of the house long enough to have a heart-to-heart with his client.

"Right. I can see where people would think that way." There was a sound of paper shuffling on the other end of the phone and Lara wondered how many other things the man was trying to do while talking to her. She had no doubt but that the call was low priority. But then, why make it?

And did he even remember his cutting words of five years ago at the kicker's sprawling fifteen-thousand-square-foot home on the West Coast?

"Good luck solving the problem," she began, ready to finish the conversation and move on with her day.

"I'd like to retain your services for a few days to see what you think of the situation, Lara." His voice was firm. Resolved. No hint of an apologetic tone here.

"You want to hire me?" She couldn't possibly work for someone with such a low opinion of her work. Someone who laughed at her technique. Someone she'd like to tell to take a flying leap off a short cliff.

"Yes. Right away. And I'm willing to compensate you well to meet with me as soon as possible since clearing up this matter is an extremely high priority for me."

"One of your clients thinks he is suffering from a curse?" She thought she'd made her boundaries clear—no help to anyone who scoffed at the problem, or the remedy.

Realigning the bottles of oil in the colors of the rainbow, Lara struggled to make order of chaos.

"No. Actually, it's me. I can provide room and board for the weekend. In fact, I'd insist on it since my home is on a remote island and we'd need to remain accessible to one another until we solved the problem."

He wanted help? The idea stunned her as her hand slid

from a bottle of eucalyptus oil. He'd been so quick to dismiss her work. Just like all her mother's self-righteous friends.

"You want to retain my services." She needed to be sure she'd heard correctly.

"Yes, as soon as possible."

Lara had to admit she was intrigued. And just a little tempted to prove the value of her skills to yet another person who didn't believe in her. Still, she couldn't imagine working for him.

"We would need to discuss this in more detail before we—"

"We can discuss it as soon as you arrive. I'm flying up to the island today and I can speak with your assistant about arrangements for you, as well. Can you be ready by noon?"

Was he insane? She looked at her grandmother's watch locket hanging from the chain around her neck, checking the time only out of curiosity since there was no way she could pack up and jet off to some—did he say island?— at a moment's notice, even if she wanted to.

"I can't—"

"Fine. We'll shoot for a three o'clock departure."

She drew a breath to tell him where to get off, but he barreled ahead.

"I'm sending your office a contract as soon as we hang up. Does five thousand for a retainer sound sufficient to at least get started, assuming you can bill the overage afterward along with expenses?"

Her mouth snapped shut on whatever protest she'd been about to make. Obviously, he was more serious about this than she'd realized. But then, something about this man tended to short-circuit her hyperacute extra senses that usually made her aware of those subtleties. She'd noticed the phenomenon the last time they'd worked together and she hadn't appreciated it one bit.

"Five thousand?" Her work had never been about the money. If anything, she took on far too much work without payment; since she couldn't turn her back on the dire-need cases that tugged at her heart. Missing women. Runaways. Worse. Five grand would nicely underwrite a few more of those jobs.

Besides, Dexter's work offer would keep her busy during a light workweek when her abilities were already turning sluggish with lack of use and exposure to paint fumes.

"If that sounds fair to you." Dexter Brantley waited patiently on the other end of the phone like her personal cash machine.

Not that she'd ask for a nickel more than he'd offered. But she would be foolish not to accept the job. Whatever humor he'd once found in her career must have fallen away over the last few years because he sounded utterly serious about employing her.

And damn it, who was she to judge what hard times he might have fallen into? The rainbow arc of essential oil bottles glittered back at her optimistically.

"That seems fair."

"Excellent." He sounded genuinely pleased and Lara found herself again recalling his features. The man might have rubbed her the wrong way five years ago, but he'd definitely been easy on the eyes. "I'll contact your office in half an hour when I've made the travel arrangements and if I don't talk to you before then, I look forward to meeting with you tonight. We can have dinner at the house. There's a chef there so you won't have to suffer through my cooking."

A chef? Dinner at his house on a remote island sounded awfully chummy, but then again, if his place was even half as big as the kicker's palatial estate, they wouldn't exactly be crowded.

"Great. I'll see you tonight." Hanging up, she called for Jamie to start making plans.

She would just take her laptop with her and compose her rebuttal to the psychics smearing her online while enroute to wherever it was she'd been hired to go.

Hell, she didn't even know what to say. But the light workweeks would only continue if the negative press about her didn't stop. Her mother's friends would drive customers away if they kept up their claims that Lara's psychic abilities would decrease the more she used them for what they termed "superficial purposes."

But she wouldn't cave to pressure from her colleagues to turn her psychic gifts into some sanctified tool that should only be employed to solve life or death crises.

She'd learned over the years that the more she utilized her abilities with psychometry and remote viewing, the more adept she grew with them and the more reliable her visions became. Like any skill, she had to exercise it frequently and she couldn't bear to use it on nonstop investigative work, even if she could afford to do so. She would burn out in a couple of years under the emotional toll if she got tangled up in one heart-wrenching missing persons case after another.

Helping the know-it-all sports agent out of a jam this weekend could be just the antidote she needed for a life

turned too dark and complicated lately. And if the more
altruistic psychics of the world didn't like her choices, they
would just have to get over it. Because Lara knew how
painful it could be to linger on life's dark side and she had
no intention of ever repeating the experience.

SHUTTING OFF the listening device his cousin had loaned
him for a few weeks, Victor Marek smiled over his latest
discovery as he kicked back in his Manhattan loft. His luck
was finally turning around.

In fact, he hadn't felt so good since he'd kicked a sixty-
three-yard field goal to win the Sugar Bowl during his
senior year.

Thanks to the wonders of modern spy gadgets available
to private detectives like his cousin, Victor now knew his
archenemy was headed to a remote island for the weekend.
Score one for Vic.

And—of all the wondrous luck—Dex Brantley just
happened to be heading there with the very same psychic
he'd somehow used to railroad Victor's career.

Until this afternoon, Vic had almost forgotten about
loopy Lara Wyland's role in his spectacular fall from grace
as one of the most dependable kickers in the NFL. Shit,
Lara had probably been on Brantley's payroll from the
beginning. She'd helped lift the curse on Vic's leg tem-
porarily, but working with her had changed Brantley's
perception of Vic. Shortly aftwerward, Vic had been ousted
from the sports agent's lauded circle of the highest-paid
athletes in the world.

Now, slipping out of his bread company uniform from
the morning's gig as a truck driver, Victor could almost

taste victory. Brantley had promised him the world, but he'd been quick to renege on the deal as soon as Vic's leg had acted up. In short order, Vic had gone from a lucrative contract with hot prospects on the horizon to a bad reputation as a health risk with odd superstitions.

He'd wound up with no contract and no future.

Vic folded up the bread company uniform and tucked it into a bag for incineration next week. Right now, he needed to make travel plans to Brantley's secluded mansion, the only property Vic purposely hadn't torched. The mouse was scurrying to the only open hole.

Victor wouldn't allow Dexter Brantley to run anyone else's livelihood into the ground. With the NFL draft fast approaching, Vic planned to step up his efforts to end Brantley's reign before he got a hold of other starry-eyed college players.

And since Lara Wyland hadn't exactly helped Vic get his career back on track after Dexter's barrage of negativity and lack of support, then as far as Vic was concerned, she deserved to go down with him.

2

FOUR HOURS INTO HER TRIP, Lara decided that if she ever wanted to disappear from her day-to-day life, the Thousand Islands would be a good destination.

The St. Lawrence River provided the international border between the U.S. and Canada over New York State, with little islands scattered throughout that used to act as a playground for the rich and famous at the turn of the century. She'd researched the area online while on board the chartered flight to Alexandria Bay, New York, before she'd caught a boat to Brantley Island, a speck she could now see in the distance as she braved the deck of the small speedboat Dexter had contracted for her trip.

Wind whipped her hair in her face, stirring up the water so that ice-cold droplets pelted her cheek, forcing her back down into the stairwell leading to the heated cabin below. The airplane pilot had personally escorted her to the boat, so she knew she was in the right place even though the captain was an old man from Quebec who mostly spoke in French.

The guy grinned down at her now and smiled as he cut the engines for their arrival. Lara hadn't brought much with her since she'd only be here for the weekend but she wished she'd brought more sweaters. She couldn't picture herself warming up anytime soon after the trip through the icy water to reach the place the boatman had called the Isle of Brantley with a rising inflection on the last syllable. It had been one of the few things he said that she'd understood.

The island was smallish compared to, say, Key West. But considering the land was privately held, it was fairly impressive. She guessed it to be at least a couple of miles wide and it looked as long in the other direction, from what she could see when they were farther away and had more of a perspective on it.

Now, as the craft skimmed quietly up to the long pier on the western side of the island, Lara only had eyes for the house that looked more like a small castle than a modern place of residence. There had to be twelve different levels in the roofline and that only counted what she could see from this direction. Turrets and porches, gables and steepled peaks dotted the huge mansion. Smaller outbuildings surrounded the main home, each one taking on scaled-down features of the larger place for a soothing sense of architectural harmony. Most of the buildings were made of weathered gray stone with dark roofs, but here and there she noticed some wooden structures, too. Two porches, a gazebo and a long bridge spanning a pond were all whitewashed cedar. There was a boathouse a few hundred yards away from the dock and a helipad perched on top even though there was no aircraft currently in sight.

In a word—wow.

This Brantley guy had to come from some serious old money to have a place like this, because homes of this kind didn't just end up on the market for your average Joe to buy. This kind of house was a family heirloom. At the very least, you had to be damn well connected to end up with a prime piece of property in a region with this level of old money prestige.

The boatman attempted to help her with her bags but she waved him away as emphatically as he waved away the tip she tried to give him. She only had one rolling suitcase and she regularly lugged around more than that at the mall.

Still, as the boat and Pierre sped off on the river, Lara felt awfully alone. There was no car in the driveway to signal someone was home. For that matter, there wasn't even a driveway. An islander probably didn't have any need for a car, but it seemed strange. The house loomed over her, quiet and…foreboding.

"Too many ghostfests, Lara," she reminded herself, wondering if she was letting her psychic sensibilities run away with her to feel a vaguely threatening air about the building. She climbed a short set of wide stairs in the walk winding its way up to the house. Sure, older homes tended to have more latent psychic energy—impressions—lingering within their walls. But that didn't mean she had to tune into a bunch of loopy ghost complaints. She should focus on her job instead.

Except that the thought of seeing Dex Brantley again reminded her of the heightened sexual awareness she'd felt around him the last time they'd met, even if she had resented him for thwarting her job. She hoped the sensation had been a fluke because that kind of sensual vulnerability could be…dangerous. Lara had to be extremely careful about relationships with men since negative emotional energy could seriously hurt her professional abilities.

Music emanated from the house as she drew closer. The sound of screaming guitars and screechy singing that characterized eighties rock seemed horribly out of place in a turn-of-the-century mansion but the incongruity chased away the sense of lurking phantoms.

Brantley must be inside.

When knocking proved futile against heavy metal, Lara turned the knob and let herself inside. She couldn't shake the *Alice in Wonderland* sensation of being too small in a big house. The door handle was mammoth and required two hands. The door itself seemed scaled more to a garage than a residence. And the foyer soared up four stories above her as she settled her suitcase inside, a domed skylight of stained glass casting colored slivers of sunlight all over the stone floor. It was like standing inside a prism and would have been an almost mystical experience if not for the drum solo blaring from upstairs.

"Hello?" she shouted into the echoing heights of the grand staircase connecting the four stories…that needed something to soften it up in her humble opinion. The endless spindles and railings called to mind a cell block more than home sweet home, but what did she know about decorating?

No doubt somebody had thought it looked good to spend such massive amounts of money on building this place.

When no one answered, she started up the stairs, following the sound of the music past a wall of paintings in the second-floor corridor and then winding around a grandfather clock toward the soft chink of metal she recognized as the methodical rise and fall of weights.

At the same time she thought it, the weight room appeared straight ahead of her. Door open, she could see the wall-mounted stereo that was the source of all the noise and a complex silver weight machine that put her host's back to her. And she knew it was her host.

The few hours she'd spent with Dexter Brantley had imprinted his physical self concretely in her brain.

Though the guy was a sports agent and not an athlete himself, he possessed a physique as rock-hard awesome as any of his famous clients. The man could hold his head up in any major league locker room.

Currently, he pumped iron in a smooth, steady rhythm, his hands gripping a bar attached to a tall stack of weights. She had a vague idea that he was working his lats, but then she hadn't been the most diligent phys ed student in school, so she might have that wrong.

Whatever it was he was working on, the results were head-turning.

"Excuse me?" She flicked the light switch on and off to get his attention.

He didn't bang the weights down, but she could tell she'd interrupted the rhythm by the way he rushed the descent.

"Lara?" He swiveled on the bench to look at her. "Did your plane arrive early?"

Looking at the clock on the wall he frowned. Her gaze followed his.

"No, but it looks like your clock is about an hour behind. Did you have a power outage?" She remained focused on the clock face until she was certain she could look at him again without letting the etched muscles distract her.

She'd felt this sexual awareness of Dexter the last time they'd met, but she hadn't been particularly attracted to him given his reaction to her work. Now, seeing him half-naked in only a pair of gym shorts evoked a more visceral reaction.

"No." Rising from the bench he threw a towel around his neck and swiped it across his face before he reached to turn the music off. "But then this house is known for its peculiarities so it makes perfect sense for the clock to be an hour off. I usually wear a watch but—" He cut himself off and extended his hand. "Welcome to the island."

She reached for his hand and she had the sensation of sinking into him. Their fingers connected and for a moment, visions assaulted her in rapid-fire succession.

"Thank you," she croaked over a hoarse voice while images and memories—his memories—flew through her head.

Such a vivid connection with another person didn't happen to her very often, but it was the occasional consequence of meeting people or touching their belongings. She had grown more skilled at shielding herself from that kind of sensory input, but she'd been so distracted by her unexpected reaction to Dexter that she hadn't focused on drawing the necessary mental boundaries before she touched him.

Now, in that brief moment of physical touch, she saw private affairs she had no business witnessing. She saw Dexter in bed with a woman, his lean, powerful body stretched over her as he brought her to a shattering climax.

The blatant sexuality of the memory, of his finesse, drenched her consciousness, igniting an answering physical response as strong as a lover breathing on her naked spine. Her knees wavered.

"Lara?" He held on to her hand, possibly sensing her strange reaction even if he didn't have a clue what exactly was going on in her head. "Are you okay?"

She wanted to speak, to reassure him she was one hundred percent terrific so he'd release her, but his continued touch only gave rise to more of the same. Only now, she saw Dexter's thoughts in regard to her—a frank male interest that undressed her slowly, his broad hands covering her nakedness before he laid her down....

"It's nice to see you again," she finally managed, wrenching her hand back before they mentally consummated a relationship they hadn't even physically begun. "I'll let you—" she gestured vaguely to his sweat-sheened body, at a definite loss for words "—clean up."

"Sure. Let me just show you to your room." He continued to eye her peculiarly as he yanked a T-shirt off one of the other weight benches.

Elbowing his way into the gray cotton, he turned left outside the weight room and pointed to another set of stairs.

"There are almost thirty bedrooms in this place so you could have your pick, but I thought you'd like this one." He pointed to a set of double doors ahead of them.

Lara kept pace with him but tried not to get close enough for any accidental touches. She was still having a hard time catching her breath after the handshake and it was all she could do not to fan herself. She'd never had that kind of psychic sexual connection to anyone before and it was an experience she'd rather not repeat with a man who was practically a stranger. A man she needed to develop a working relationship with.

Damn it, she needed a glass of ice water.

"Anywhere is fine," she assured him as he tugged open the wide doors.

"Great. I'll grab your bags for you while you make yourself at home." He waved her into the most beautiful bedroom suite she had ever seen.

French doors opened out onto a terrace she could see between plum-colored drapes which had been pulled back to show the view of the river. A wide-open space made the room feel enormous, but part of that might have been because of a simple decorating scheme composed of dark wood furnishings and parchment-colored walls featuring small frescoes on alternating panels around the room. The paintings were rich with gold leaf and vibrant colors depicting scenes from life on the river. Historic boat races, riding parties on horseback and notable nearby homes were all memorialized on the walls.

A four-poster bed sat off to one side of the suite while a private bathroom connected to the room on the opposite wall. Lara wanted to duck under the covers and seek refuge until she pulled her head together but already she heard Dex's footsteps on the stairs.

"Nonsexy thoughts, nonsexy thoughts. Think nonsexy thoughts." She tapped her forehead as if to work the message in deeper. When she quieted, she stared hard at the four-poster.

And promptly had a vision of a young man and a

woman tangling naked limbs on the mattress, their cries of ecstasy as real to her as her own breath.

"Oh God." She shut her eyes against the onslaught of imagery even though she knew that wouldn't help.

Images of the blonde's arched back and fingers fisted into her pillow assailed her along with the realization that the bed linens she'd seen in her vision were different from the ones on the mattress now. For that matter, the skirt hiked up around the enraptured woman's waist looked like a period costume with its billowing underskirt in a soft white cotton.

Carefully, she pried her eyes open again only to see Dexter enter the room out of the corner of her eye, still looking extremely buff in his gym clothes. He set her suitcase down by the door, muscles flexing admirably.

"Is the room okay?" He was really a great deal more polite than she remembered from their last meeting, but perhaps that was only because he needed her help now.

She would try hard to remember that and not get sucked in by the devastating mixture of he-man good looks and charm that was probably completely fake.

"Actually, do you mind if I just take a quick peek at whatever nearby bedrooms you have?" Hadn't he said there were thirty? She didn't mean to be picky, but if there were ghosts hanging out in this room, or at very least, someone else's old memories, she would rather not contend with them in the bed where she hoped to sleep.

His brow wrinkled for only a moment before he waved her through the double doors.

"There are a couple of other possibilities down this hall. Are you sure you're okay? You look a little…flushed."

Yes, well, witnessing Dex's sexual memories as well as the carnal history of her bedroom tended to rouse a woman's color.

"It must be from the wind out on the river." She touched her cheek and felt the warmth penetrate her cool hand.

He paused outside another door and opened it, revealing a smaller bedroom with deep blue curtains drawn against the daylight.

"I can have it made up for you in just a few minutes if you'd like to switch. The woman who helps me keep the place in order is still onsite…"

Lara lost the thread of conversation as she stared at the bed with old-fashioned velvet drapes hanging from its wooden canopy top. Her mind's eye saw a maiden's bare leg slide through the fabric as the sound of masculine laughter reached her ears. The woman moaned from the other side of the drapes, a man's feet peeking from the curtains as he obviously knelt in front of her and Lara knew she was somehow tuned in to the home's sex frequency, a psychic trip down each bedroom's memory lane.

Maybe it had all been jump-started by her surprising physical reaction to seeing Dexter working out. Her latent hormones had sprung into overdrive at the first ripple of muscle.

"That's all right." Laura took a step back from the cries of mutual completion within the room. "The room you set up for me is just fine."

"Really, it's no problem to—"

"Honest. I was just curious to see more of the house, but I'm sure we can do that later." She held up a hand as if to say she would not argue the point, but truth be told, she just needed for him stop walking in her direction so she could shut down the inappropriate thoughts. "I'll see you at dinner."

She regretted the perplexed look on her host's face, but it was better to appear eccentric than sexually obsessed.

"We're eating early—six-thirty. My chef wants to be home before the bad weather comes."

"Perfect." Returning to the first room she reached for the door to insert a barrier between them. Her legs felt weak and her breasts tingled with as much awareness as if he had just circled ice cubes around her nipples. "I'll see you then."

Closing the door, Lara sank to the floor with her back to the hallway, unsure how to rein in her thoughts enough to get through the weekend. She was here to solve Dex's problem, not create more drama with her visions. Maybe if she meditated for a while she could raise the mental barriers she needed to close out the strange energies vibrating through the house.

Through her.

Because no matter how much she'd like to write off the whole strange chain of events this afternoon as psychic occurrences inspired by an old house with a history, Lara knew that her unexpected attraction to Dex had stimulated those passionate visions. It was an uncomfortable fact, but one she'd have to work around because nothing would make her walk away from this job and all the good works she could finance because of it.

Besides, this weekend had become an opportunity to prove to uppity psychics everywhere that there were many valid uses in the world for their unique skills, whether it was finding a lost child or dispatching negative energy. Psychic gifts were meant to be shared, not hoarded for preconceived agendas.

Hauling herself to her feet, Lara unpacked her suitcase while trying to shut out the sound of the blissful couple making it in the bed nearby. She'd sleep on the floor if they didn't disappear by bedtime.

But first, she had to survive this dinner without melting into a puddle of lust at Dexter Brantley's feet. If this strange psychic sexual energy didn't disappear on its own tonight, she'd have to find some way to do her job without having the sports agent anywhere near her.

3

DEX HAD GROWN ACCUSTOMED to his life being totally un-
predictable and weird in the last year since his luck had
turned to crap. But sending a beautiful woman running
brought him to a new all-time low.

What the hell had gone wrong in his meeting with Lara?
Sure, he should have kept better track of the time so he
could have greeted her a little more professionally, but was
it such a crime to be shirtless?

Dressing for dinner after his shower, Dex buttoned his
shirt and went the extra mile with cuff links to make up
for the sweat show earlier. Lara couldn't walk out on this
job. He didn't expect her visit to accomplish anything
concrete with his bad luck, but he needed her to quiet the
media about Dex's Hex. Once he spread the word that a
psychic investigator had shown up to banish the curse,
hopefully the interest in a very stupid story would die
down.

He had just threaded his second cuff link when a knock
vibrated the door of the master suite.

Lara?

He opened the door to find his chef on the threshold, a
burly New Englander who looked more like one of Dex's

prizefighter clients than an expert on French cuisine. His apron was smeared with dirt and he held a dilapidated assortment of plants in a tray of clay pots in one hand.

"I quit." Chef Roy thrust the plants into Dex's hands before he reached for a suitcase at his feet.

"What?" Dex was pretty sure he was gaping like a caught fish.

"I cannot work like this any longer." A crate at Roy's feet jangled with loose pots and pans as he jostled it. "My salmon delivery did not arrive because the boatmen won't come out to a cursed island. I burned my arm on a flare-up from the stove. Then the pots fell down from the hanging apparatus and—"

"Roy, don't do this." Dex noticed the burn on his forearm looked pretty bad, but the guy didn't seem too banged up from the pot rack giving way. "You're the ace on this staff, the go-to guy for crepes, the least superstitious of anyone who works here."

"Yeah? Well that's not saying much since I'm one of the few people left making the trek out here." The chef shook his head with what seemed to be genuine regret, but his lower lip curled down stubbornly as if daring Dex to argue with him. "And I would stay if I could get through a regular day without being thwarted in my job at every turn, but *this* was the last straw."

Roy snatched back his plants from Dex's hands and a few dead leaves fell to the hardwood floor as he waved around the browned foliage.

"Your plants died?" Dex knew he must be missing something since Roy wasn't some prima donna athlete who cut and run at a little patch of bad luck.

"They are my prize-winning herbs!" He raised his voice, clearly serious about the plants being the last straw. "They are the envy of every gardener and cook on the St. Lawrence. The cuttings are sought after. The plants take first prize at every regional fair for their health and beauty—"

"What happened to them?" Dex lifted a drooping leaf and wondered how he'd ever feed his guest without Roy. "Maybe if you gave them some water—"

Roy's wheezing noises cut him off. When he finally got himself under control, he tucked the plants under one beefy arm and shook his head.

"No. They have suffered the blight along with the rest of the indoor herb garden. I do not wish to be superstitious, sir, but I cannot work in an environment so full of bad luck. Today I burned my arm, tomorrow I might cut off my thumb. Today my plants die, tomorrow my dough might not rise. The things that happen here, they don't make sense."

"Roy, come on. I've got company here for the weekend. She's a psychic who's going to fix this whole curse thing." Dex shrugged into his jacket, seriously debating tackling Roy if he tried to leave.

"When she does, you call me. But I will not wait around to end up in the E.R. or have my reputation of excellence blighted as surely as my plants. Sorry, Mr. B. I put out the salads and the bread. That is all I could offer anyway without the salmon."

"But—"

Roy shook his head. "Good luck with the house. You should warn your lady friend this place is dangerous."

The surly chef stomped away, towing his suitcase on wheels and cradling his diseased plants.

"She's not my lady friend," Dex called after him as the chef bounced the suitcase down a flight of stairs toward the foyer and the exit. "She's a nationally renowned psychic investigator. And when she cleans up the curse, I'm going to be swimming in applications for that chef position."

By the time he got to that last bit, Roy and his plants were well out of sight, the banging suitcase echoing up the stairway as he descended to the main floor.

"Well damn." Dex didn't bother going back inside his room for a tie. He figured Lara Wyland would be more impressed with having food to eat than the sight of Hugo Boss's finest silk, so he stalked toward the stairs intent on the kitchen, hoping against hope that Roy had left behind something besides a couple of bowls of lettuce for what might be the most important dinner of his life.

No woman—not even a super hot fake psychic—could be expected to work on an empty stomach.

"Dex?"

Her voice called out softly to him from the floor above and he looked up to see her peeking out of her bedroom suite.

"Wow." He slowed down his march to the kitchen to admire the view with what he hoped was suave subtlety and not out-and-out lecherousness. "You look great."

Descending the stairs, she wore a thin, silky dress in a cheetah print. Wide straps outlined the square neck and the skirt was sort of full. Her brown hair matched the base color of the print. The whole effect was kind of wild and sweet at the same time.

The curves outlined by the dress veered more to the wild side, however. Who knew she'd been hiding such a spectacular bod the last time he'd seen her? He'd thought she was hot five years ago—if a little crazy—but he hadn't imagined this. Back then, he'd just caught a few of her sizzling glances and spent half the day envisioning her reading his X-rated thoughts.

"Thank you." The color deepened in her cheeks and he suspected she'd read his mind a little too well.

For that matter—damn.

He might have succeeded in laughing off her psychic claims long ago, but maybe there was something to her abilities. He'd called her in a moment of total desperation earlier, not sure what else to try. But afterward, he'd figured out a way to get his money's worth out of her visit even if she proved to be a fraud. He was just about to quiz her regarding the exact nature of her perceptions when she closed the bedroom door behind her and joined him in the hall.

"I heard you arguing with someone a moment ago. Is everything okay?"

"Nothing is okay. My chef just quit and that's only one of many incidents I can claim in the last year that support the idea of a curse, but first I need to ask you something."

He offered her his arm and she took it after the slightest hesitation. She rested her fingers lightly on the sleeve of his jacket, as if she didn't want to rest any weight on *him.* Once again he got the impression that she wanted to flee.

And didn't that suck for his ego? He knew he couldn't make a pass at the woman he'd hired to help him out of this, but it irked him to think she would be wary around him, especially when he couldn't take his eyes off her.

"What would you like to ask me?" She moved down the endless stairs with him easily, her brown suede pumps obviously not giving her any trouble.

His eye traveled the length of her leg in appreciation and he wished his hands could take the same route.

"Can you explain to me exactly what skills you claim as a psychic?" He noticed her eyes skim over his chest and he smiled to himself until he realized she was probably just thinking he had a piss-poor dress code—first no shirt, now a suit without a tie.

"I claim several skills, but I don't ask anyone to believe in them. I thought when you called me you had moved beyond skepticism." Her tone was cool, and he remembered this brusque side of her from the last time they'd met.

Damn it, he probably hadn't made a very good impression then. But what the hell had Victor been thinking to hire a psychic to cure his crappy kicking stats? Dex equated it with the same reaction he would have had if he saw one of his NBA stars going to the hoop with a necklace of garlic to ward off vampires. It seemed fairly hysterical…at least until you were the one living a nightmare.

"I'm sorry. I didn't explain myself well. I don't mean to sound skeptical, I just wonder what sort of—I don't know—*powers* do you tap into to be effective in your job? Do you read people's minds?"

That was the main thing he wanted to know. Could she see inside his head to those moments when he had very slyly mentally undressed her? She couldn't be acting frosty toward him because of that, could she? It was rude but had to be commonplace for her. Kind of like breathing for a guy in his age bracket, right? He didn't indulge the hobby often, but around Lara he felt that he didn't have a choice. The woman was seriously hot.

When they reached the first floor he steered her through the foyer, his body aware of her every move as her dress brushed his pant leg. He guided her past the formal dining area into a smaller, private room where he preferred to eat. The decor was a little more subtle here and Roy had at least set the table for two and lit a long row of white candles.

"Reading minds isn't normally a specialty of mine." She stopped in front of a chair and peered around the room. "Your chef did a beautiful job for a guy on his way out the door."

The candlelight played off her hair, the setting far too romantic when he needed to talk business. *Thanks, Roy.*

"Yeah. Assuming we like *salad*." Dex figured he'd starve to death in no time in keeping with his run of bad luck.

"But there's bread," she pointed out. "And it smells fantastic."

"Roy makes his baguettes from scratch." Dex moved to pull out her chair. "Have a seat and I'll at least get us some wine."

He caught a hint of her perfume as she settled herself in the high-backed chair, a citrusy note that coaxed a keen physical response even though he was sure he'd never smelled the fragrance before. The temptation to lean in for a better sniff was strong. He'd have to be careful around her this weekend since he seemed to be hanging at the end of his personal rope in a lot of ways lately. God knew he might not have the kind of reserves needed to maintain his distance and he couldn't very well afford to get involved with anyone now when his life had morphed into a nonstop catastrophe.

"So no mind reading?" He wanted to clarify that point.

"It happens occasionally, but it's not a talent I've tried to cultivate." She folded her napkin in her lap and wouldn't meet his gaze.

Should he be worried?

"What about my mind?" Asking pointed questions was his business as an agent so he didn't hesitate to get to the heart of the matter with her now.

He'd fantasized about having her ten different ways in the past five minutes so if she could read minds, she would have been treated to one hell of a show.

"Any thoughts I pick up from you or anyone else are random accidents that I shut out wherever possible because that feels like too much of an intrusion to me." She watched him steadily now and he read the underlying message.

She'd picked up the sexual vibes from him.

Before he could make excuses for his, er, *detailed* thoughts, she hurriedly changed the subject.

"But let's talk about why I'm here. We didn't get into specifics on the phone, but I'll admit I found it surprising you would contact me after our last meeting. I didn't get the feeling you were very impressed with my methods."

"It wasn't your methods I took issue with. It was Victor's absolute belief that his grandmother could put a curse on him for forgetting her birthday. Sorry, but that sounded like paranoia setting in and he'd had a track record of not taking any responsibility for his performance as an athlete." Dex opened the door to the wine refrigera-

tion unit built into one wall and checked over the selec-
tion. "We've since parted ways, but in the last month or
two I had cause to remember that visit you paid to him
because I'm having a few problems of my own with a supposedly hereditary curse that affects the Brantleys."

"I'm listening." Lara shifted toward him in her seat, her
breasts pressing against the neckline of her dress in a way
that made him realize how badly he needed a drink if he
wanted to survive an evening across the table from her.

"Actually, if we're going to get into this now, would you
mind walking this way with me?" It was rude to seat a
woman at the dinner table and then yank her away, but he'd
feel better about his story if he had some cold hard
evidence to back it up. "We can grab a better bottle of wine
from the stash outside the kitchen and I've got a memorabilia room I think you'll need to see in order to properly
appreciate the kind of year I've had."

Setting her napkin aside, she rose. "As much as I appreciate the offer for dinner, I'm very ready to get down
to business."

Her hips rolled with her walk and as she drew near, he
was tempted to stick his whole head in the wine cooler to
drag his temperature down a few degrees.

He shut the door to the small refrigerator and gestured
to a hallway off the side of the dining room opposite to
where they came in. Time to cop to his cockamamy story
and see if she could do anything to help or if he would have
to rely on his Plan B for making use of her psychic talents.

Whether or not she could cure the curse, hiring Lara
Wyland would at least be a good publicity move to coax
back some of the superstitious players. He would fax out

a press release Monday morning saying a noted psychic had tamed the curse and given him two thumbs-up for his luck to return.

Hell, just having this incredibly sexy woman in his house made him feel a little luckier already. He drew a deep breath to redirect his thoughts before he started mentally undressing her again.

"Okay, let me start by saying that I came into the business of sports agenting in an unusual way. I helped a friend who was about to turn pro negotiate his contract while we were in university and made an explosive debut in the market." He'd always thought he was just smart about his job, but this year had taught him that smarts definitely weren't always enough. "Other agents called me a lucky bastard and griped about the killing I was making as the new kid in the business. But six lost athletes later, I'm referred to as 'Dex the Hex.'"

Lara wound through the cavernous hallways beside her host, trying in vain to get a fix on this man and what he wanted from her. Part of her still wondered if he was pulling some kind of elaborate hoax to see if she'd fly to the ends of the earth for the sake of a job he considered quackery. But he was different from the last time they'd met. She could tell from the more somber set of his whole face and the way he treated her. The lightheartedness she recalled—mostly at her expense—had vanished.

"I'm sorry if I find it difficult to take that too seriously considering your personal chef, your private island and a home that would probably be termed a castle on any other continent." Coming from a two-bedroom house in the suburbs, it was tough to feel empathetic toward this man whose ill fortunes of late clearly hadn't impacted his lifestyle.

"Don't be deceived, Lara," said Dexter, walking past a huge, industrial-looking kitchen before he paused in front of an even bigger wine cooler than the one in the dining area.

Reaching inside the specialized refrigeration unit, he seemed to be searching for the right bottle of wine.

"Don't waste the '86 Bordeaux on me. I'm not enough of a wine enthusiast to appreciate it."

He yanked his head out of the refrigerator to gawk at her and she realized she had just pulled the kind of stunt that always freaked Jamie out.

"How did you know the vintage—"

"Sorry," Lara said, keeping the focus on the business at hand. "Why not just take a light, recent Pinot Grigio and tell me about this curse?"

She grabbed a corkscrew and two glasses off a nearby bar rack while Dex found a bottle he liked, still shaking his head.

"Okay. But I think it would be better for me to show you what I'm talking about instead."

Juggling the bottle and the glasses he insisted on taking from her, Dex walked her down yet another corridor to a room labeled by a simple gold-plated sign, The Athletes. He opened the door with his elbow and sat the wine bottle on a table just inside.

She walked in behind him and handed him the corkscrew. The room radiated "guy" and looked like a mini sports hall of fame. There was Astro Turf on the floor instead of carpet and at one end of the space there was a putting green. The walls were the main attraction, covered with press clippings, framed photographs and jerseys from every big-time sport. The whole place smelled faintly of cigars and she had the impression that the room had been used for entertaining the athletes it had been dedicated to, or at the very least, sports fans.

"I used to call this my Jock Stock Room, because the athletes who are in here were my bank portfolio." Dex uncorked the bottle and poured them each a glass of wine. "At the end of the nineties, long-term, hundred-million-dollar contracts were in vogue for all four major sports. I was the agent for ten of the top-earning twenty-five athletes. Ten percent of their income was mine."

"Was?" She sipped the vintage appreciatively, thinking that even with her low-budget tastes she could get used to living like this.

In her opinion, Dex Brantley was still a damn lucky man.

"Yeah. The good news is I've managed to keep four of them." He pointed to a small segment of one wall with two basketball players, a baseball player—a pitcher, she thought—and a football player. "The bad news is even these guys have performed poorly and have since negotiated contracts that wouldn't land them among the top ten thousand earners in sports. Some high school kids with sneaker deals earn more."

Lara would bet they still earned a lot more than her, but she understood Dex would only see a percentage of that and he had a bigger company to run.

"What happened to the other six?"

"Well, before one of the New York papers christened me with 'Dex the Hex,' there was 'Dex's Hex.' The lucky bastard standing in front of you once represented the top earner in NASCAR, soccer, Major League Baseball, the National Football League, the National Basketball Association and the National Hockey League. I had all six inked to nine-digit deals, more endorsement offers than we could handle, and each athlete hadn't even reached the prime of their careers." He pointed out another section on the wall and over there the names were more recognizable. One guy wore a Yankees uniform and she was pretty sure that team was famous for spending big on their players.

"The six-hundred-million-dollar man?" Now this sounded like a tidy sum.

"Well, ten percent of it, at least."

"So where are they now?" Lara quizzed, intrigued by his world.

"Let's see…the race car driver found God in, of all places, a car wreck, and dropped off the face of the Earth. My world-renowned soccer star starred in a world-renowned homemade porn tape with a teenager, which didn't exactly endear him to his sponsor, McDonald's. You know how many times I've been mocked by the 'I'm Lovin' It' jingle?"

"So one athlete's extremely poor judgment and another's religious awakening are a curse to you? I'm not buying it," Lara said.

"Fair enough, but allow me to proceed. My star slugger loved belt-high fastballs almost as much as he did dirt-biking across sand dunes in the Mojave Desert. Well, he didn't see one coming."

"A fastball?"

"No. A sand dune. He jumped one, but didn't notice another just behind it, crashed his bike, busted his shoulder, and lost his powerful swing. In baseball, contracts are guaranteed, so ordinarily it wouldn't be a huge deal. However, the Yankees had asked for a clause in the contract prohibiting him from dangerous activities, specifically dirt-biking, as they knew of his hobby."

"Three down." Lara stepped deeper into the room to see the next guy on Dex's wall. "But that's simply bad luck."

"Here's more for you. In football, there are no guaranteed contracts, so if you're injured and can't play, there's no paycheck for you. What you get in a signing bonus is all you're ever guaranteed. My star quarterback opted for a huge, long-term, incentive-laden contract that would have easily inked him in excess of one hundred million if he could stay healthy for five years. He stayed healthy for exactly five minutes. A blindside hit to the back of his knee tore a ligament and he never took another snap."

Lara winced in empathy. *Poor guy.*

"What about your hockey and basketball players?"

"An injunction filed against the National Hockey League led to the courts ordering my Russian hockey star back to his hometown, voiding his contract. My NBA guy is currently serving five-to-ten for shooting a police officer."

It was Lara's chance to reverse the roles the two had played in their prior meeting. In their original encounter, Dexter clearly had been appeasing his kicker's wishes while dismissing Lara's psychic abilities as mumbo jumbo. Now Lara could write off Dexter's situation as simply bad luck, bad judgment and bad timing.

"That is a miserable turn of events, I'll grant you that, but—"

"That's exactly what I thought at the time. But I wasn't

worried because I always had the devil's own luck and I knew I'd just rope in the next promising crop of athletes. Except that right about that time, a small regional weekly paper did a story about my run of bad luck along with a hodgepodge of historical research into my family and the Brantley curse that supposedly kicks in for any guy in the paternal line when he turns thirty-three."

Now it was getting interesting. She wasn't sure if the chill on her skin came from a moment of precognition that things were about to get worse, or if she merely shivered from his proximity. Her physical attraction to him had been fairly well masked for the last half hour, but the closer they stood, the more strained her defenses became.

"How old are you?"

He lifted an eyebrow and didn't answer. He didn't have to.

"So the author of this newspaper story thought the curse had kicked in for you?" Her eyes strayed to the open collar of his shirt where he'd neglected to place a tie. She glimpsed a hint of a long silver chain that disappeared into the fabric.

Immediately, she had a vision of a woman underneath him, nipping at a small medallion that hung from his neck with her teeth. She tried to banish the image, but then she realized the woman wasn't some unknown stranger from his sexual past.

It was her.

She was just flat-out fantasizing.

"The author was a charter member of the local historical society and a former friend of my grandmother's. She thinks everyone cares about crazy old stories from the past." He drained his wine as if he hoped the drink would brace him. "I never guessed she'd be right about that, but the story was picked up by a national newswire and appeared as a feature piece in papers all over the country last October."

"So there really is a curse?"

"A self-fulfilling prophecy more likely. Athletes are extremely superstitious. Five more of my clients deserted within the month. They weren't top earners, but their defection made me realize people were buying into the hex thing. I can't negotiate a good deal for my existing clients in an industry that bought into the Curse of the Bambino and respects a winning streak like it's some kind of divine miracle."

Dex waved his arm to show her the five other athletes who ditched him.

"Maybe if I could talk to the woman who wrote that article?" Lara needed to investigate the historical angle of the curse to plan a strategy to help him.

By now she was convinced that Dex was sincere about wanting her help even if she wasn't certain he respected her methods any more now than he did back then.

"I'm hoping to arrange that before the weekend's over. But first let me tell you what happened after the article came out and a whole new crop of guys left me hanging." He stalked back to retrieve the wine bottle and poured her another glass.

"Only if you think it's relevant. For what it's worth, I believe you." It was more than he'd offered *her* five years ago.

"My administrative assistant quit, my bookkeeper embezzled $24K from the company, the elevator in my Manhattan office building broke with me on it for twelve hours during which time I missed a meeting with the hottest new athletic prospect I had all year. Then my Aspen ski chalet caught on fire the week before my New York apartment caught on fire. All that was capped off with a nine-car pile up on the George Washington Bridge that all but totaled my car."

For a moment she was too dumbfounded to speak. What had started out as a business crisis had snowballed into a chain of events that would have made any sane person lose their mind.

"If there is a curse on your family line, Dex, I'll help you find it." She made the promise easily, and with renewed certainty that this was an appropriate use of her talents no matter how much he paid her. He deserved help. "But have you ever considered that someone might just be out to get you?"

She had an immediate vision of a man fighting, a man who was angry. Drenched with sweat and fury, the anonymous man lurched forward—toward—Dex?

Lara was about to relay this quick vision, when Dexter turned toward her, setting his drink on a glass case full of autographed footballs. Laying his hand on her arm, he spoke quietly. Emphatically.

But she had no idea what he was saying since his touch had caused a psychic shock of outrageous proportions.

Any awareness of the angry man disappeared as the mental pictures she'd experienced earlier in the weight room returned. Dex in bed with a redhead. Dex backing a blonde up against the same football case they were standing near right now. Dex sneaking a woman into a locker room to let her live out a naughty fantasy.

"Please." Lara couldn't handle the images of his past that mingled with a strain of attraction to him she couldn't repress. Her breath came in shallow gulps and she realized her heartbeat was twice as fast as normal.

"What?" He looked confused and…aroused?

Afraid of what might happen next if she didn't get herself under control, Lara pried his hand off her arm.

"The touching sets off my psi abilities and makes me see…"

She didn't know how to let him know. She still held his hand in midair, or did he hold hers? It was impossible to tell in the middle of the room, breathing each other's exhalations and standing far too close.

"What do you see?" His voice scratched along her senses, teasing her with a hungry quality that robbed her of reason.

"It's never happened to me before, but I can see all your sexual thoughts."

4

DEX WOULDN'T HAVE BELIEVED Lara's claim a few years ago. Hell, he might not have believed her mind-reading abilities a few months ago.

But since then, he'd had reason to suspect there were powerful forces at work in the world he didn't understand, something beyond bad luck, something that could explain the fantastic mess his life had become. Plus, right now, Lara's flushed face and lightly trembling hand made one hell of a strong case for her allegation that she could tap into his thoughts. She didn't look much like a woman who'd been having a platonic conversation. With her fast breaths and softly swollen lips, she appeared to be in the throes of some major sexual fantasies.

"You're kidding." He watched her steadily, thinking maybe he should put her claim to the test.

Mostly he'd hired her as a visible public bandage for his hemorrhaging good luck. But if she really could read minds, maybe he could put that talent to more use than he'd realized. Just for fun, he thought of something very graphic that he'd like to do to her.

She nearly jolted out of her skin a split second later. Her whole neck went red and she looked as though she wanted to take cover behind the nearest trophy case.

Holy hell. She hadn't really just plucked his X-rated thought out of his head, had she?

"I don't understand." He hooked an arm over a rack that held darts and extra foosball pieces for the table in one corner.

They'd been in the middle of a serious conversation before she sprang this on him. And yet—he never would have suspected her of putting the moves on him after her obvious reluctance to work with him.

"I don't, either." She released his hand and took a small but noticeable step away from him. "I thought I could work around this—um…problem—but it started the moment I walked into the weight room today and saw you working out."

He couldn't suppress a grin. "Maybe you were just overwhelmed by my virility." She was turning him on in a big way just talking about this stuff. He would forget all about his bad luck if this line of discussion continued. "Honestly, do you think it's just some form of…attraction gone haywire?"

Some women were really good at picking up vibes from a guy—psychic or not. Just because she could sense those thoughts didn't mean her whole psychic gig was legit. There were defensive players in every sport who could practically "mind-read" an offense. That didn't make them psychic. Maybe Lara's talents ran in that direction. She was empathetic. A good reader of human nature.

"Definitely not." The pink tinge of her cheek deepened, but he didn't know if that indicated pique at his suggestion or possibly embarrassment at having her attraction laid bare.

She wrapped her arms protectively around herself and then paced a few more steps away as if thinking.

"Because I'll admit that my mind has been taking a few

sexual side roads ever since you arrived." He didn't want her to think she was alone in this. He could barely get his thoughts back on business.

"I *know*." She quit her restless roaming to shoot him a level glare. "I had hoped to avoid acknowledging that I could sense those thoughts because that seems like an invasion of privacy and it's also counterproductive to a working relationship."

Ah, damn it. Now he was the bad guy.

"What can I say? I'm used to behaving like a gentleman, but I can't be the first guy you've ever met who didn't *think* like one." Like clockwork, he pictured himself undressing her.

She rolled her eyes and he wondered if he was more oversexed than the average guy.

"It's not that." Lara pushed her fingers through her dark hair in an impatient gesture. "I can usually tune out that kind of stuff easily—like I told you earlier—but I've been bombarded with sexual images ever since I walked in here today."

He pulled over a stool from the miniature bar at the far end of the putting green and wondered if he also should guard his body language a little more closely so she couldn't pick up those cues.

"Meaning?"

"Meaning I'm picking up more than just random physical attraction stuff." She moved closer, but only to retrieve her wineglass for one long swig—and then another. "I'm also seeing snippets of your sexual past."

He definitely didn't need to see that turned-on, melting look come over her face again.

"It's because of this freaking curse, isn't it?" He didn't even want to think about what the hell she might be seeing in his past. He stared at the electronic dartboard and hoped that would help him maintain mental privacy. "Instead of you and me putting it to rest, it's going to be my luck that you run screaming because some crazy mind's eye trick of yours has you visualizing every chick I've ever been with."

This year had tested his limits, but by God, if the negative karma started to infiltrate the bedroom…

"No." Her hand reached to cover his, a fleeting, cool touch before she retreated again. "I shut it down as fast as I can. And it's nothing detailed, just moments of…did you really sneak a woman into an NFL locker room?"

"Holy—"

"Sorry." She apologized right over his curses. "I just wanted to give you a taste of how I'm being mentally bombarded and it's even more intense when you touch me."

He remembered that's what had precipitated all this— she'd sort of spaced out when he'd been discussing the wealth of enemies one made while in the sports agenting business.

"I'll be careful not to get too close again." A crap solution to the problem as he wouldn't mind getting *very* close to Lara Wyland. Since he'd hired her mostly as a publicity stunt they'd have a lot of free time this weekend. He would spin out the whole story of his screwed-up year in case she had any insights, but he didn't plan to hold séances or anything weird like that.

There would have been plenty of time to indulge an attraction.

"But I don't know if even that will clear up the problem." Stalking away from him again, she picked up one of the putters from a golf bag at the end of the green. "Because I'm also having retrocognitive visions of the whole sexual history of the house."

"What?" His voice notched up a disbelieving octave. She had to be putting him on. But if she wasn't…damn, this *was* an old place. How many encounters could there have been over the years? Even if he didn't totally buy into her retrocognition or whatever she'd called it, the notion alone set his senses on overload.

"Remember how I wanted to change rooms earlier?" Her short fingernails scraped lightly over the leather handle. "It was because I could see a couple from a century ago having sex in the bed."

"Lady, I tried hard to put aside my disbelief to call you this morning. But you can't possibly expect me to think—"

"Want me to prove the truth of my visions?" Twirling the expensive titanium golf club like a baton, she planted it on the turf and eyed him again. "Need more details on the blonde you backed up against that trophy case over there? The redhead you—"

Christ.

"Okay." He drew a hand across his throat in the universal gag order. "I believe you."

And damn it, how did she know all that stuff?

When she was quiet for a long moment, he polished off his wine—little help that proved—before filling in the silence.

"I hope you know you're freaking me out over here."

"I'm pretty well freaked out myself." She blinked hard and jammed the club back into the golf bag. "This has never happened to me before."

It wasn't until then that he stopped to think about what that kind of experience must feel like for her.

"Never?" He had to be sure of that, needing answers to process, information to analyze. He'd never been the kind of guy to go on gut instinct, preferring solid data in his decision making.

Something he guessed he'd be hard-pressed to find with Lara.

"Never even close. I've occasionally seen into other people's intimate thoughts accidentally, but not to this degree. And not to the extent that I can't shut them off." Her palm came to rest on her pink cheek and he realized she must be trying to cool her skin.

She was overheated and flustered. And even if she might be frustrated by the onslaught of sexual images, she still seemed to be…turned-on.

The idea tormented him since he really shouldn't act on it. For the course of the weekend, she worked for him, even if there would be plenty of downtime for getting to know each other better. Hitting on her put her in an unfair position. And he didn't want to spread his streak of bad luck by drawing her any deeper into his world. The chef had gotten burned—literally—and had feared further bodily harm. While Dex might have minimized the seriousness of Roy's fears earlier, he damn well didn't want anything to happen to Lara.

"How do you recommend we handle this? Besides making sure we don't touch." He hated the boundary that imposed. Even if he didn't plan to seduce her, there was always the small possibility that something more could happen. She was a very attractive woman alone with him in his house for the weekend. The idea he couldn't go near her already made him twitchy.

Especially since she'd ratcheted up the temperature between them by relating her visions.

The more he thought about *that,* the more he seemed to think about her. She had a body that would take any guy's eye and serious guts to tough it out in a profession where cynics like him gave her a hard time. And the way she was looking at him through her lashes right now…she had him ready to back her into the nearest dark corner.

"There has to be something to take the edge off this feeling." She glanced up at him quickly, seeming to catch how that sounded. "I mean, I need to find a way to diffuse the overload of distracting…thoughts."

Dex studied her face under the recessed lighting strategically placed to highlight his glass trophy cases. Lara appeared hot and bothered, uncomfortable and irritated.

Basically, she exhibited all the signs of being sexually frustrated. And she would be alone with him for the weekend. Him. The guy who had been too busy staunching rumors of a curse to even go out on a date for the last six months, let alone take someone home with him.

Every one of those months felt like a century right now, and Dex couldn't help the conclusion that blared into his head with all the subtlety of a rookie in his first contract negotiation.

"Maybe we're thinking about this the wrong way." Spurred out of his seat by the idea, he approached his sexy guest before he could talk himself out of what he had in mind.

Her fingers toyed with the ends of a black silky scarf tied in a bow around her waist. Or at least, they toyed with it until he stepped right into her personal space. Then her fingers' nervous rhythm stopped all together.

"What do you mean?"

The jump of her pulse at her throat spurred him on and suddenly he wondered why it would have ever occurred to him to let them both suffer alone.

"It's not helping for me to *not* touch you." He paused a scant few inches from her, even though he kept his hands to himself.

The scent of her citrusy perfume teased his nose along with another fragrance—a warm musk that acted on his senses like an aphrodisiac times ten. The scent of her arousal.

Her brow scrunched in thought as if she was attempting to figure out some complicated algebraic equation.

"You can't be suggesting…"

Damn it, he wanted to do more than suggest.

"Maybe we're running from the obvious solution." His hands already itched to touch her, his fingers flexing at his side with the effort to restrain himself. "Maybe all that misplaced psychic energy just needs a physical outlet."

She shook her head, but her whole body trembled in response to his presence. Her tongue darted out to wet her swollen lips.

"Trust me, men know what it's like to deal with the physical consequences of ignoring sexual needs." He reached out to touch her, but let his fingers hover over her shoulder so that the final choice belonged to her. "I might be able to help you."

The heat of her body captivated him, rooting him to the Astro Turf next to her so that he couldn't walk away if he wanted to. He couldn't remember the last time he'd desired a woman this much.

"It's not a sexual need." She remained stubborn, her lush lower lip curling down in an all-out pout. "And if you're suggesting I sleep with you so that I can do my job better—"

His hand fell to his side again.

"I don't imagine there would be much sleeping involved. I just thought it might help us both think more clearly, since right now, I'm guessing there's only one thing on our minds."

Lara stared at the gorgeous gray-eyed guy in front of her and counseled herself to take shallow breaths. A deeper breath might involve inhaling the scent of his aftershave, a risk she couldn't afford in her worked-up condition.

"I didn't mean to share my tense state with you." She wouldn't go so far as admitting that maybe sex with a man she barely knew would help her unease, but with her body responding so strongly to Dex's presence, she had to wonder if he had a point in suggesting she find release.

He shrugged with lazy, masculine grace, his suit jacket shifting against his body with a silken swish.

"I'm still hoping we can put it to pleasurable use and end all of the agitation." His eyes roamed over her freely now, even though he hadn't let his hands do the same. His thoughts teased at the corners of her consciousness. Fragmented images of his hands stroking down her spine, his mouth pressed just below her ear. Were those his thoughts or hers? She couldn't be certain of anything other than the arousal coursing through her.

She would cave if he touched her. She knew it, and she guessed he knew it, too. But she respected that he wanted the decision to be hers in the end, and damn it, she couldn't let a bout of overactive psychic sensual energy sway her into making a bad mistake with Dex.

I can make you feel so good.

Lara thought she heard Dex's words out loud for a moment before she realized she'd plucked them from his head accidentally. He was thinking about what he would do to her if she let him….

I can give you the longest, hottest, sweetest orgasm of your life, guaranteed to shake the living hell out of any negative vibes inside you….

She heard his thoughts as clearly as she heard her own. But worse, she could see him giving her that promised orgasm in his mind. In her mind.

No more fragmented images for her. This moment, his intent flowered through her brain in splashy Technicolor. He had her bent backward over a table, his feet planted between her legs while he drove deeper inside her. Her arms wrapped around his neck, her fingers clutching at his back to hold on.

"Oh God." The epithet floated from her lips with a tortured moan and she seemed to sway toward him in spite of herself. "I don't want you to think I'm some kind of sex-starved lunatic."

That fear was the last remnant of sane thought she clung to, a powerful desire for acceptance no matter the seeming craziness of her psychic gifts. She didn't ever want to hear his mocking laughter again.

Dex's gaze zeroed in on her lips and the heat she saw there mirrored what she felt inside.

"If you don't think I'm crazy for investigating a century-old curse, believe me, I won't hold it against you for trying something unorthodox to help me solve my problems."

Most likely they were both crazy, but she didn't think she could walk away from him. Besides, she used her psychic skills wherever possible to prevent an eruption backup of strange energies, and she worried that if she didn't give this latest psi meltdown an outlet, she wouldn't be able to help Dex at all. She might even hurt her abilities long term.

Whatever was happening to her was serious and unprecedented. She'd had relationships with guys blindside her psychic abilities before, but they'd never short-circuited onto an all-sex frequency before. She needed help.

"I—" Words failed her even after she made up her mind. She knew his touch would set fire to her whole body. Now she just hoped the flame could burn away all the strange visions, leaving her clearheaded again.

"Let me help you, Lara." His whispered words hummed across her senses and buckled her knees as she fell against him.

"Yes."

His arms went around her instantly and the contact made her cry out with pleasure. Relief. His mouth slanted over hers and her head dipped back in complete submission.

The growling noise he made in his throat reverberated through the kiss as his tongue stroked over hers. His touch bombarded her with sensory images—his sensual wants and fantasies. But that lasted only a moment before her own hunger grew stronger than any fluke psychic ability.

Heat burned in her, scorched through her veins, her limbs, her core. Dizzy with need, she fastened herself to Dex, his body a strong, solid anchor in a sea of sensation she couldn't navigate. She fastened her lips tighter to his, hungry for the warm connection.

His hands skimmed down her sides, sealing her to him with deft pressure. Her breasts to his rock-hard chest, her belly to taut abs, her hips to the steely length of what she needed most.

He pulled back from the kiss, his eyes narrowed with purpose.

"I need to take you somewhere else. Somewhere with no sex memories for me."

She heard the words but didn't process them until he swept an arm down behind her knees and tugged her off her feet. A small squeal of surprise eked out from her throat, but she wound her arms around his neck for the ride.

They'd reached a point of no return and she'd committed herself to follow this heated madness wherever it led.

Ducking her head into the hollow between his neck and his shoulder, Lara traced her tongue along his collarbone while he assured her he knew a place where she wouldn't see as many memories.

She couldn't imagine a corner of this old house that hadn't seen plenty of carnal activity, but he carried her up one set of stairs and down a short corridor. She didn't look up until they crashed through a set of double doors and into a huge, circular room with a bank of curtained windows.

Dex angled her near the wall.

"Move the first switch up just a little bit." He nodded toward a row of switches and knobs.

When she did, small gas torches leaped into flame in a half-dozen candelabra ringing the walls. The effect was so pretty and old-fashioned, probably an original feature of the home built—according to her boatman—at the end of the nineteenth century.

"This is beautiful." Heavy gold draperies lined the windows with some kind of silky, champagne-colored sheer curtains behind them. That lining blew gently along the floor as a storm kicked up outside, rattling the doors slightly as wind battered the huge house.

She realized there were no visions of sexually engaged people here, just an intense awareness of the man who held her in incredibly strong arms.

"You're beautiful." He set her on her feet, his gray eyes as dark and stormy as she imagined the river must be outside.

Her heart pounded at his intense perusal.

She caught new psychic undercurrents here, a frustration deep inside him that he'd kept veiled under good manners and a host's polished charm earlier. All at once she understood he needed this—her—as much as she needed him. The knowledge soothed that lingering voice inside her that told her she was foolish to wade in so deep, so fast with him.

That understanding drove her hand forward to touch him, her fingers skimming down the front of his pressed shirt.

"It's better in this room," she confided as she tunneled her fingers inside his shirt through the narrow spaces between buttons. "Thank you for bringing me in here."

She didn't know how he'd known this place would be psychically quieter, but she didn't care about finding answers now. Her fingers couldn't stop roaming over him, making quick work of the buttons to open his shirt to the waist. She savored the feel of doing whatever she pleased to this man who had once intimidated her.

He reached out to her, cupping her face in his palm. The touch made her heavy-lidded, her head tipping toward his hand like a flower to sunlight. His other hand landed on her shoulder, fingers nudging aside one strap of her dress so the fabric hung limply off her arm.

Her breath caught in her throat as she looked up at him. He was a tall, powerful man. Six foot three or four. Supremely well built. He could have taken her against a trophy case downstairs easily and she wouldn't have minded.

She had wrapped herself around him like a twist tie on a bread wrapper, yet he'd brought her up here. Helped her to find her footing before she threw herself into sex with him.

Did he know his actions only made her want him more?

"Take me." She whispered the words with a heartfelt plea since she couldn't take control here. Her senses were too overloaded, her thoughts too scrambled with visions, feelings—and deep, hungry need.

"With pleasure." He reeled her closer, one hand skimming down the zipper on her dress as he walked her backward toward the bed.

She willed her clothes off and he seemed to read her

mind, flicking her other dress strap off her shoulder so that her outfit floated to the floor in a silken heap. Her strapless bra hugged her breasts too tightly, the Lycra and lace annoying when she only wanted Dex against her skin.

She tried to reciprocate, shoving his shirt and jacket off his shoulders. Luckily, he'd undone his own cuff links, so she was able to strip him of the clothes without too much trouble. And thankfully, she was able to shut out his fantasies now and just live the reality. Or maybe she'd become his fantasy.

The mini torches silhouetted his body in golden light and shadow, casting exaggerated emphasis on his ripped muscles and taut sinews. She traced her fingers over the indents that defined each ab, each rock-solid plate that would provide supreme control to a man in the act of lovemaking.

Her calves hit the bed at the same moment the thought blitzed her brain and she tipped back into the soft mound of a goose down duvet. The pad of feathers shifted to accommodate her while Dex loomed above her, hand on his belt.

She watched in sweet fascination as he tugged the leather free and unfastened his trousers. Her hands grew impatient to touch him but he was out of reach. When she stretched up to stroke his thigh he redirected her fingers to her own body, dragging the tips across one hip to the waistline of her panties.

The wicked man.

She obeyed the unspoken command, trailing her fingers over her belly and just barely into the low waistband. His dark eyes followed her every move, spurring her on to twist the black lace around her hand and tug the material downward. With a shimmy of her hips she eased the panties lower. Lower.

Her gaze dipped down to check his progress on his trousers just in time to see his boxers hitch on a massive erection. A small cry escaped her throat, and she reached to touch him, feel him, stroke him into doing what she wanted.

He stretched over her, arching to retrieve a condom from the nightstand. She realized fleetingly that this must be his room, and marveled that the sexual impressions would be so muted in her mind, here of all places. But then he pulled her panties off her legs and she forgot to think.

He kissed her full on the mouth while his fingers settled between her legs. Sparks lit behind her eyes. He drew her tongue into his mouth and sucked gently, making her hips twitch in automatic response. She drenched his hand with her want, but he didn't come inside her yet.

Instead he broke their kiss and made himself comfortable between her thighs. The kisses he gave her there made the mating of their mouths look tame, his tongue now administering long, vigorous strokes. She arched back, her hips reflexively thrusting forward. Clearly he knew exactly what to do to elicit a strong response and she could hardly regret the other women who'd populated his life and his memories before tonight. Dexter Brantley gave her the most powerful orgasm she'd ever had in her life, her pelvis contracting so hard she twisted in the sheets with it, her fingers gripping helplessly for a hold on something before she slid into sweet, pulsating oblivion.

She barely had time to recover herself when he loomed over top of her, his boxers gone and his sex sheathed and ready for her. Her cries of fulfillment melded into a new cry of delight at the way he stretched and filled her.

Delirious with the feel of him and the sensations he inspired, Lara could only cling to Dex, trusting him to bring them to new heights with each strong thrust of his hips.

Her eyes rolled back as he slid into her, the pleasure made all the stronger by the slow withdrawal. She wriggled beneath him, ready to take charge and give him the same kind of soaring bliss he was giving her, but he held her fast to maintain control.

And heaven help her, she couldn't argue with someone who made her feel so…amazing. So ripe with lush sensuality. She swore he must be some kind of mind reader, too, that he could tell exactly what she wanted.

He pinned her wrists over her head, stretching her out to his gaze and his touch. But mostly he seemed to just want to keep her still while he brought his thrusts to a new level, picking up the tempo until her breath came in soft pants.

The air in the room changed, becoming electrically charged. The doors rattled with the wind and the curtains danced while the torches swayed from the drafts. Lara couldn't staunch the growing tightness in her womb, the coiled pleasure just waiting to untwine with the slightest—

"Aaah!" She was free-falling into sweet spasms again, her whole body reverberating with the forceful waves of pleasure.

Dex stilled above her, his cock lengthening impossibly inside her before he, too, couldn't hold off his orgasm any longer. His whole, beautiful form shuddered with the strength of it, his hot chest coming to rest over hers even though he let go of her hands to prop most of his weight off her.

Lara's whole world tipped with the recognition of what

had happened between them. Sex hadn't just been physically incredible. It had connected them on a psychic and emotional plane she doubted Dex would ever admit.

She hadn't just trespassed on the employer-employee boundaries by sleeping with him tonight. She'd been an active participant in their worlds colliding. And while she would make every effort to ensure they could proceed with business as usual in the morning, Lara had the feeling nothing would ever be the same between them again.

5

HAVING AN AFFAIR with a woman who worked for you—a woman whose help you really, really, needed—was a dumb move.

But having an affair with a female employee who could also read your mind—that ranked right up there with stupidest ideas ever. Still, as Dex watched Lara slide from his bed at five in the morning, her long, pale limbs visible in the dawn light that penetrated the curtains, he found it impossible to regret the decision.

She slipped out into the hallway and he wondered if she would be coming back or if she was returning to her own room. She hadn't bothered to take her clothes with her, instead pilfering one of his shirts to wear for her trek through the house.

He sat up, more unsettled by that thought than any potential regret about getting involved in the first place. What if she saw more visions? As much as he'd enjoyed the results of her exposure to the sexual images, he didn't like the thought of her seeing snippets of his past intimate encounters in the house. Not that there'd been a huge number, but still…no one wanted to share that kind of thing with a new—

What? Weekend lover? The label didn't seem big

enough to cover the monumental experience of the night before. He thunked his head back into the pillow, trying to get comfortable and knowing he wouldn't. His life was imploding and everything he touched seemed to make things worse.

The idea sent him bolt upright in bed as worry for Lara suddenly gripped him—

She screamed from somewhere in the house and he vaulted off the mattress, yanking on his boxers as he ran.

"Lara?" He shouted for her in the hall as her scream faded.

"I'm here." Her voice echoed and bounced off high ceilings, telling him she must be in the foyer or on the main staircase.

"Are you okay?" He skidded on a throw rug, more than a little freaked out that he'd started worrying about her safety seconds before she began screaming.

What the hell was that all about?

"Yes." Her voice hovered above him as he reached the stairwell and he saw her slumped midway up the steps to the third floor. Her face looked paler than the white marble under their feet. A dark purple nightgown reached to her calves and he realized she'd gone to her room for clothes at some point.

"What happened?" He took the steps two at a time to reach her.

"I went to get a robe and brush my teeth." She tied the belt of a purple terry cloth bathrobe, covering the silk nightgown he'd glimpsed beneath it. "And when I came back down the steps, I saw this couple arguing on the landing. There."

She pointed to where he'd stood a moment ago on the

second floor where a balcony overlooked the first-floor foyer.

"You saw people?" He tried to keep the skepticism out of his tone as he wrapped an arm around her shoulders. "You mean like in a vision, the way you saw people yesterday?"

"I guess so." Her nose crinkled in thought, drawing attention to the lightest freckles imaginable spattering the bridge. "But when I saw them, they appeared more vivid. I really thought they were there."

She shook her head, obviously upset and confused. He tried to lead her down the stairs but she didn't seem to want to move.

"And they weren't having sex like the people yesterday?"

"No. They were yelling and furious with each other." She clutched the robe tighter and peered back down over the railing again as if the pair might still be there. "But I guess it must have been a vision since they were in period clothes. The woman had on a gorgeous dress with yards of skirts and he had a tall hat like he'd just gotten home from a business trip."

Dexter stilled.

"How would you know that?"

Lara scanned the foyer with her eyes.

"Just an impression. Or there might have been suitcases by the front door. I don't know."

He didn't like where this was headed one bit.

"What was the argument about?"

"She said something about his faithlessness and not being here the next time he came home. Then he—" Her eyes went wide as she turned to him. "He shoved her down the staircase."

"What happened next?" He didn't bother to hide the flatness of his tone then, having heard this story all too many times already.

"I don't know. That's when I screamed and you came out. I looked back up to him and he was gone. By the time I glanced down the stairs, I didn't see her anymore, either."

He released his hold on her shoulders and sank back against the stairs, the cold marble freezing against his butt through the thick layer of his cotton shorts.

"Then you're robbing this story of all the best parts. Because it was after she fell that she screamed her curse out for the whole house to hear, telling my great-grandfather that his whole life would go to hell from that day forward, along with all his descendants." He looked up at the family portraits marching up the wall lining the staircase.

"That's how your family's curse began?" Lara relinquished her spot at the banister and sank down to the step beside him.

"It was great-granddad's thirty-third birthday. His mistress was pissed off after hearing rumors that he'd met someone else during his trip to New York so she told him they were through. One of the maids said she cursed him louder with each step she hit on the way down."

"There was no maid." Lara shook her head immediately. "They were alone. And that poor woman didn't say anything while she was falling. I'm surprised she lived through it, let alone could speak after that tumble."

She looked so disturbed about the incident, Dex could almost imagine she really had witnessed some significant part of his family history. But he'd stretched his willingness to believe by buying into her mind-reading capabilities. He could buy Lara psychically tuning into the house's sexual energies since there'd been hot chemistry between them from the moment she'd walked into his weight room yesterday. Surely that kind of sexual awareness could manifest nonstop sex thoughts. That combined with a little mind reading—a phenomenon that didn't stretch his beliefs too much since he'd lost to enough poker players who seemed to have a gift for reading other people—Dex could handle.

But it was tougher for him to accept that she might be able to see…ghosts.

"Don't you think maybe you're reading too much into the house's history?"

"I don't know anything about the history other than what I've seen and what you just told me, so I'm not sure how to answer that."

He didn't want to debate the issue. But the effort to suppress a response was too much.

"Well maybe you've heard some rumors about the family curse? Maybe an Internet search on the plane?" He stared down at the foyer below where splashes of moonlight played over the hall's pale stone tiles. "Not that there's anything wrong with studying up on a client—far from it—I'm just suggesting maybe you're not seeing your visions clearly if you've been swayed by tales from the locals. I heard the facts about the curse straight from my own grandfather, so I feel certain that I've got the story straight."

Lara stiffened, her shoulders squaring beside him.

"First of all, I didn't read squat about your family

history—I'm just reporting on the incident in that hall that scared me enough to make me scream." She rose from the stairs to glare down at him where he sat. "Second, I was under the impression that you hired me to hear about my experiences in this house and around you. Remember, it was *you* who wanted me here."

"Wait." He hadn't expected his comment to be such a source of contention. But then, he couldn't pretend to understand how someone like Lara would react to his present situation.

Her bare feet slapped up three more steps away from him before she turned.

"In fact, I'll be glad to refund your down payment on my services in full if you'd be so kind as to call your boat back for me to leave."

"No." Things were definitely out of control now and he supposed he could see her point. His words had come out differently than he'd intended and now he'd hurt this amazingly giving—and hot—woman.

He couldn't let her leave. For better or worse, this woman represented his last hope to reclaim his life.

Lara's whole body vibrated with indignation as she faced down the man she'd slept with a few short hours ago. How could he go from giving her the most amazing sex of her life to wounding her feelings and her pride with his suggestion that she'd hunted up tidbits about his family to use in her work here? The thought riled her, although perhaps the incident was a good reminder of why she should never give a man too much power over her.

Some mistakes were too devastating to make twice in one lifetime.

"I'm sorry, I must have misheard you. Did you just refuse my very polite request to refund your money in exchange for passage off this island?" Just because she was psychically gifted didn't mean she would be this man's—or anyone else's—laughingstock.

She took enough crap from her mother's friends. She wouldn't make herself vulnerable to a gorgeous sports agent with the Midas touch in the bedroom.

"Yes, you misheard me." He swiped a weary hand through his hair, the motion bringing one bicep and tricep into advantageous view. "I only want to tell you that I will not accept a refund and that I really need you to stay. But I'm happy to discuss this at length this afternoon after we're both dressed and fed and—better rested."

She didn't know if it was the tiredness in his voice or the nearness of his hot, mostly naked body that swayed her. But she found herself less eager to leave even if she wasn't beating a path back to his bed.

"I can't have my professional integrity questioned every time I turn around if I'm going to help you." She needed that much to be clear. "And while I appreciate you—er, helping me get through a rough patch last night—I think it would be best for us to resurrect some working boundaries under the circumstances."

Dex nodded. "I totally understand and agree. Thank you for staying."

She hated the contrary sense of letdown she felt that he hadn't even argued with her on that point. But maybe he thought sleeping with her had been a mistake.

He walked back toward his room and she followed.

"Let me just get my things from your room."

Together, they traveled the same path their feet had taken the night before in a frenzied rush. Now, the melancholy she felt seemed to echo through the house and she had a sudden sensation of relationships going awry here for a hundred years.

"Are you sure you'll be okay in the guest suite?" He opened the door to admit her. "What if there are strangers in the bed? Ghosts or something?"

"They're not *ghosts*." She retrieved her dress and undergarments from the darkened room. "They're impressions from the past—leftover memories that very few people would ever be able to see."

Her skill made her special, damn it. If she hadn't been barraged by critical e-mails and harangued in well-read industry blogs recently, Lara might have enjoyed writing an article about her experiences at Brantley House for one of the psi publications. Their field was only going to be as smart and respected as the people who chronicled it.

But that was out of the question for at least the next few weeks, after a local politician had admitted to visiting her for occasional tea leaf readings. You would think she had committed a federal offense from the outcry among the more "serious" psychics, her own mother included. Of course, her mom had been looking for subversive ways to mold Lara in her own image for three decades running. But this was the first time she had encouraged her friends to do battle with Lara in a public forum—a psi Web site with a large following now receiving a record number of hits.

No way could Lara cop to ghost sightings for a little while, not if she ever wanted to work with the local police department again. Her mom's cronies would have her credibility shredded to nothing.

"Okay." Dex released a pent-up breath. "Impressions, then. Are you sure you'll be all right sleeping in that room with a bunch of fornicating impressions in bed with you?"

He brushed a hand over her shoulder, an unexpected contact after the terse words exchanged in the stairwell. She longed to read his thoughts, to gauge what he hoped to convey with that brief caress, but under the circumstances, she didn't think that would be playing fair.

"The room was quiet when I went back for my robe." She'd been surprised by that, but she hadn't witnessed a single sensual memory in the house this morning either, just the fight on the stairwell. "Maybe—maybe our being together last night helped my mind to block out the sexual frequency."

Shrugging, she felt his fingers shift on the terry cloth, his warm palm heating her skin straight through the barrier.

"Then it wasn't such a bad thing." His thumb sifted through her hair to skim a touch along her bare neck. "Sorry for doubting you back there. The bad luck has made me cynical and edgy."

"You were cynical five years ago." She wouldn't let him get away with pawning off fake excuses. "And I wasn't kidding about the need for boundaries now."

She stepped out of his reach even though her heart ran faster from just that brief contact with him.

Nodding, he moved toward the bank of windows to peer outside.

"I wasn't cynical back then. I was angry at Victor for

wasting your time when his kicking problems didn't have squat to do with any curse from his grandmother."

Curious about the gray darkness even though dawn had broken, Lara joined Dex at the window, careful not to touch him. She might have won the battle for boundaries for now, but she knew she would be the first one to cave if her hand brushed up against lean male muscle or if her nose caught a hint of his aftershave.

"That's being cynical in my book. You could only deal with the guy's downward spiral if you could attach it to some tangible fault of his own. The idea of anything cosmically awry scared you."

The view from the windows was incredible. The water churned below a narrow balcony just outside two sets of double doors. In the distance, she could see the turrets of another miniature castle on another island in the river way. She even spotted someone attempting to navigate a small boat through the rough waters. But the man soon disappeared as fog rolled over the water to encompass the buildings nearby.

"I just think people need to be willing to take responsibility for their actions and their failures. I believed that about Victor then, and I believe that about my situation now. I'm grateful for any help you can give me with this thing, but bottom line, I don't believe in ghosts or impressions, or whatever the hell you've decided to call them."

She turned to meet his gaze at the same moment the wind picked up outside. A great moaning gust blew against Brantley House and the doors to the suite slammed shut with a bang. In quick succession, doors throughout the home banged closed. A great cacophony of slamming shook the walls, rumbling through the floors and rattling Lara's nerves.

Even Dex appeared—freaked.

"I don't know, Dex." She hugged her robe closer in the chill breeze floating through the home. "Sounds to me like your local spooks aren't too pleased to go unnoticed."

SHE'D BEEN MESSING with his head. Dex knew that as he stomped around the perimeter of the grounds in the rain that had started washing through the fog about an hour ago. The weather hovered just above thirty-two degrees, the drizzle carrying the threat of sleet. For now, the haze remained thick over the river, but he could hear the waves lapping near his feet as he stalked out to the boathouse, even if he couldn't see the water below the dock.

No doubt it amused Lara to see him wig out over a house full of doors slamming in conjunction with his declaration that he didn't believe in ghosts. But damn it, that was still a coincidence. Now, when it came to all his best college football players getting antsy with his bad luck streak in the weeks right before the NFL draft—if she wanted to call that a supernatural act of fate or demons or succubi, he'd agree wholeheartedly. There was no way in hell this latest catastrophe his career could be of his own making.

His cell phone rang for the tenth time this morning and he picked up just as he ducked out of the rain into the shelter of the towering boathouse meant to store two sailboats with masts intact.

"Hello?" He dripped onto the display screen that was too foggy to read the caller ID.

He'd been getting disconnected all morning; the cell service here was wiggly at best and really unreliable on days with weather like this.

"Dex, you need to call Massimo Ortiz. He's getting—" The service cut out on his assistant's voice.

Massimo was Dex's top college football player, a guy most sportswriters predicted would be taken before the fifth round in the draft next month.

"Is he okay?" Dex shouted into the phone even though logically he knew shouting wouldn't do a damn thing. Either the service worked or it didn't.

He heard a few other snippets of Trish's words, but not enough to make sense of what she said. Something about Victor Marek?

He had to have misheard the name. The kicker had been pissed for months after Dex let him go, but he hadn't come around the offices for almost two years.

"Did you say Victor? Victor Marek?"

He was more concerned about Massimo since the kid was his future, but by then Trish had been cut off completely.

Damn it.

He pocketed the phone and was planning to return to the house to call Massimo from a land line until he noticed a rope had come loose from one of the speedboats in the back of the building.

Jogging around the perimeter of the structure, Dex dodged the lift mechanisms that kept all but two of the boats up out of the water this time of year. Since he needed to keep some vessel available for trips back and forth to the mainland, he usually left two speedboats in the water this time of year. One of them now floated far from the slip, its back end dangerously close to crashing into the vessel docked beside it.

He hauled the fallen rope out of the water, the frayed length still tied snugly to the slip. He expected to see the rope had broken or come loose from a poorly tied knot.

He didn't expect to see the thick nylon hacked through neatly, the fibers snipped in half by determined sawing from a sharp blade.

He felt damn sure none of Lara Wyland's ghostly "impressions" had the wherewithal to carry a pocketknife. Some real live person had been here, vandalizing his property, purposely trespassing on one of the most remote pieces of property in the U.S.

Maybe Dex's bad luck wasn't all in his head after all. The idea pleased him for about two seconds.

Right until he remembered that the same person who torched his two other homes might be walking around this one at this very minute. And Lara was up at the main house all by herself.

6

Where was Dex?

Lara peered out the window again, wishing she could see through the rain and fog for some sign of him after their terse words. She tried to analyze her unwieldy emotions, not sure what precisely had her most upset.

Something felt off today, as if a cloud of negative energy had descended on the island. Could it be the storm? Dex's curse? Or just her own fears about getting involved with a man who had little respect for her work?

Hugging her sweater tighter to her body, she passed a billiard room and what looked like a study, but she didn't take much pleasure from the antique furnishings or the cherry woodwork that kept the corridor dark but beautiful. Instead, she tried to logically pick apart her sense of unease so she could put it aside enough to do her job.

A shuffling noise in a nearby room startled her.

"Dex?"

She tried to get a read on the sound, traveling the hallways with her mind, but came up oddly blank. Normally, her senses thrived on those kinds of exercises, but today she felt blocked. Could her mother's predictions of her psychic failure be coming true? She shuddered at the thought, resisting superstitious thinking as much as Dexter.

"Dex?"

When no one answered, she continued to explore the house until he returned. Pausing outside a library of unbelievable scale at the end of one wing, Lara leaned a shoulder into the doorframe and admired the soaring shelves of leather-bound books in the round room of high windows and stingy lighting no doubt meant to preserve the paper. She'd bet there wasn't one volume dealing with anything remotely supernatural on those walls. This room would reflect Dex Brantley's upbringing, his response to the world.

Although...somewhere along the way, one of the Brantleys must have believed in the curse to have generated the idea in the first place.

Curious, she walked over to a shelf and pulled out collections by a dozen nineteenth-century American poets, reprinted medieval histories, works of philosophy and astronomy, books of gardening advice and treatises on modern art. The closest she came to finding anything resembling psychic intelligence was a Jungian work on the collective unconscious, an idea that got much less attention than his more traditional psychoanalytic theories.

Good old Jung.

But really, could she hold it against Dex that he took such a skeptical view of her work? He represented the predominant American consensus. They lived in a culture built on tangibles. Not many people bought into psychic impressions, negative psychic energy, precognition or retrocognition. They bought into e-mail and camera phones,

401Ks and stock portfolios. Perhaps she needed to cut him some slack and lose at least a little of the defensiveness she'd worn all her life.

"Lara." Dex's voice echoed from somewhere down the hall.

The swell of emotions she'd been fighting all morning surged with new focus. At the root of her feelings was this man and the fact that he'd helped her through a time of frightening psychic intensity. Even if he hadn't understood the phenomenon she experienced, he'd at least recognized her pain and desperation.

Some of her frustrations seeped away.

"I'm in the library," she called down the echoing halls, her voice bouncing off the cherry wainscoting and old landscape paintings that looked as though they had all been done by the same amateur artist. A family member, perhaps?

Footsteps loomed closer and closer until she spotted him.

And although she might feel off her game today, he appeared to be a hundred percent on his. Clean shaven and well dressed, Dex looked rested and ready to take on the world. Lara wasn't sure how people with gobs of money seemed so much better dressed in khakis and a T-shirt than the rest of the world, but it seemed like an immutable law that Dex followed along with the rest of his ilk even though his T-shirt was rain-spattered.

"Are you okay?" She nodded, and couldn't help but think he would be kissing her right now if she hadn't insisted on drawing some boundaries between them. "Have you seen anyone else around the house this morning?"

He slowed to a stop as he entered the room and she noticed he seemed tense. Anxious.

Then the import of his question penetrated her brain.

"I haven't seen anyone." But she might have heard someone. Should she tell him as much and risk not being believed? "Why?"

She told herself she would have sensed a person if the noise had been linked to a human being. It had probably just been the wind.

He threw himself onto a padded bench ringing the room. "I found one of the lines to my boat cut this morning. There's no way we can call that bad luck when it's so clearly been done purposefully. Someone's obviously been skulking around the property with bad intentions."

A chill skittered down her spine.

The tense set of his mouth made sense now and she realized that her ability to read Dex had quieted today since she hadn't picked up this news from him on her own. She knew from all-too painful experience that was how her relationships worked. She could read the people she was involved with so vividly at first and then—if, heaven forbid, she liked someone—she would become blinder than a bat once her emotions became involved. Her psychic abilities still worked, but her visions were more fractured about anything regarding the person she cared for.

And now, it apparently wasn't just her emotions in danger. Their safety might be compromised because her psychic skills were impaired. How would she know if someone was lurking around the house when she was distracted by her emotions and a bit psychically impaired?

It was precisely this type of phenomenon that her mother had never understood. Lara's gifts were different, hardwired into her emotions in a way that her mom's weren't. That was yet another reason Lara couldn't accept all of the most dire-need cases to use her skills. Her heart went through the wringer every time. While she wouldn't ever stop using her talents that way, she would burn out if she didn't diversify.

Shoving away old baggage, Lara tried to think on a more logical level.

"Maybe someone simply wanted to steal your boat." She moved to sit a few feet away from him on the polished leather, a safe enough distance, but one where their voices wouldn't bounce around the walls and get lost in the high ceiling. "It could be part of the bad luck streak that your property attracted thieves."

Dex frowned, obviously not liking her take on the incident. And frankly, it didn't seem likely to her either. What kind of random thief would run around Brantley Island in this kind of weather? She had a sudden flash of vision—a man cutting the tie when he couldn't unknot the rope. A tall man in a red jacket.

She focused on that vision even as, in the back of her mind, she heard Dex speaking.

"Perhaps. But the island isn't exactly accessible to your run-of-the-mill thieves. Somebody would have to be fairly damned determined to target this particular boat when the river is full of them. But I suppose the house would look tempting to a burglar." He shook his head. "Either way, I called the police on the way up here, but they can't come until the storm passes. They didn't think a thief would stick around in this weather."

"Can I see the rope?" She wanted to touch the boat tie before she lost the moment of retrocognition.

"I left it outside. It's wet and heavy and the police should probably see it in the boathouse in case it's evidence or something."

"I should go take a look." Moving toward the door, she struggled to hold on to the vision she'd had of a man sawing away at the thick tether in the boathouse. If only she could see his face.

Could this man be responsible for more of Dex's problems? Maybe this job was truly for the police instead of a psychic. The idea pleased her until she realized she would probably embrace any theory that meant she could take the first boat home where she could recover her extra senses and escape her mixed feelings for Dex.

"Hey." He reached for her arm, holding her back. "The rain is starting to freeze and there's supposed to be a hell of a storm. If the cops won't brave the weather to look at the thing, I don't think you should, either."

The vision started to fade as soon as Dex touched her. She didn't know what worried her more—the fact that his touch had such a dramatic impact or the fact that a clue was slipping away too fast for her to hold on to it.

"But they have to travel by boat. I just have to walk outside."

"The walkways around the water are extremely treacherous in this kind of weather. Water washes up over them and can freeze in an instant. I'm not about to let you go."

The finality of his words should have comforted her. He was looking out for her safety, after all. But even this small kindness made her heart clench and her head fear she was developing more feelings for him, feelings that would only blind her.

The winds outside picked up, howling in the silence between them. The sound of the gusts seemed magnified in the big old house that provided such a huge obstacle and so much surface area for the rain-laden wind to whip against. The leaded glass dome at the center of the roof only amplified the noise.

Her vision of the man in red had faded, too faint and far-off for her to recapture. Sighing, she returned to the bench where they'd been sitting. She couldn't deny feeling a greater sense of security at Dex's side.

"Fine. But I can't just waste the day waiting for the storm to blow over. We might as well tackle the work we planned this weekend so we don't go stir-crazy." She needed some kind of constructive task to occupy her since—even with the threat of her gifts malfunctioning—she couldn't help but enjoy being next to him in the dim library. The scent of leather and man provided a damned powerful aphrodisiac.

Besides, the sight of his muscular thighs in soft twill made her restless with memories of their night together. That just might be the most effective distraction she'd ever experienced.

"I can't really put you in touch with the features writer from the local paper since the satellite connection is out for the Internet and the phone lines have been hit-or-miss. I can't reach my office or one of my clients who apparently really needs to talk today." Frustration etched into his forehead, furrowing lines above his brow as he sank back down to sit beside her.

Join the club. Her physical senses crawled with unease in the absence of more intuitive abilities.

"That means you can't follow up on the fire investigations at your other homes, either." That had been high on her list today since no psychic worthy of the name would hunt for supernatural causes without making sure the earthly possibilities had been eliminated. "But we can backtrack to a question I asked you last night before the, um, stray energy forces got the better of me."

Some of the lines eased from his face as he smiled with predatory pleasure.

A bolt of answering longing shot clean through her.

"What question was that?" He leaned closer as if to hear her and her nerve endings danced in anticipation.

At least she wasn't seeing his every sexual thought today.

"Do you know anyone who might want to destroy the business you've built? Or anyone who holds a personal grudge against you?"

He slumped back again, the wall of bound volumes behind him catching him as his shoulders shoved books deeper onto the shelf.

"How long have you got?"

She lifted a brow.

"No, I'm serious. I could be listing people all day long. Other agents I beat out to represent prime talent. Clients who turned sour when they didn't get the deal they wanted with their top pick team. Hell, I even managed to make enemies locally and I'm usually only up here a month out of the year. It takes a special personality to tick people off with such regularity."

Concerned, she told him about the flash of a mental picture she'd had of the man sawing the tie to his boat.

"But you didn't see his face?" Dex asked when she finished relating the visual snippet.

"No. But I think it was the same man I envisioned once last night when you were talking about enemies. I saw an angry man in a fight, or perhaps bracing for a fight." She fingered the quartz beads on her necklace, wishing for more clarity in the scenes. "Have you had a fight, a physical fight with anyone lately?"

"Besides a Turkish cabbie and a New York cop? No."

Confused, she waited for him to explain.

"Never mind. And no, I haven't been in any real fights since I was a kid. I'm not sure what you're seeing. Do you think the person you saw might have been an athlete?"

She concentrated, trying to recover a clearer memory of what she'd already seen.

"I can't be sure." She would study the faces in his trophy room later today and see if any of them sparked a memory. "How about if we make a concrete list— names that we can cross-reference with some of the most malicious incidents to see if there are any common-alities?" She understood how his success could tick off his peers. God knows she'd had a taste of that herself recently with the outpouring of ill will from the people who should support her the most. "But who have you crossed swords with up here? Anyone who might have had access to your boat?"

"I doubt it." The lights overhead flickered for a moment and Dex paused to look up. "The people around the islands who are ticked off with me are a handful of history pres-ervationists who want to include this house on their tour list. They don't understand why I don't want a bunch of camera-wielding tourists photographing the place every day in the summer. I don't mean to sound like a snob, but this isn't just a family heirloom for me, this is where I go to get away from everything."

Lara nodded, understanding. Even without her heightened sensitivities, she would be able to tell Dexter was a man who lived on the edge, a man who needed a retreat to keep his sanity. She planned to ask him more about potential enemies, but her attention was drawn strongly to a volume on a bookshelf across from where she sat.

The book in question was red leather with faded gold lettering on the spine. Some decorative pattern on the spine beneath the worn title made the work an attractive piece. Losing focus on whatever Dex was saying now, she rose from her seat to retrieve the book.

As she closed in on this suddenly compelling volume, the title became clear.

The Brantleys in the Thousand Islands.

Reaching for the massive tome, she became aware of Dexter behind her. Freeing the book from its place on the shelf, she made an effort to focus on him. To hear what he was saying since his lips were moving, his expression concerned.

"…heard anything? And what is that?"

Lara shook off the fog of the strange moment, unsure what had drawn her attention so suddenly to the weighty tome in her hands.

Dex touched her shoulder, his hand grounding her in the here and now.

"Are you seeing ghosts again?" He studied her as if she'd lost her mind, his eyes searching her face.

"No. But I might be hearing them or—responding to their wants somehow." She knew that sounded crazy, but she couldn't worry about sounding like a whack job in her line of work. Maybe now that she'd fully alienated her mother, she would be able to delve deeper than ever before in her work.

Success always involved risk. Perhaps she should remember now that she was freer than ever to accept that.

"And they wanted you to—stop listening to me and start reading a good book?" He glanced down at the cover for the first time and his expression changed. Hardened. "Ah. The ghosts are nagging you to free them from their century-long captivity by reading their horrifying tales, right?"

Five years ago, Lara had let that kind of comment worm its way under her skin. Now, she took it at face value—a snarky remark from a frustrated guy who didn't have all the abilities she possessed.

That didn't bode well for their relationship—working or otherwise—but she was done hiding her light for the sake of other people's comfort.

"I brought a whole set of unique talents to the table when you hired me, and one of them is going to involve listening to whatever this old house has to say. Haven't you ever wished the walls could talk?" She gestured to the soaring shelves before taking a seat with the family history book. "Well lucky for you, now that I'm here, they can."

FROM HIS POSITION on a second-story balcony, Vic peered down into the library of Brantley House, his feet sliding out from under him while the couple inside nearly steamed up the windows with the looks they were giving each other.

Brantley and the sexpot psychic were definitely an item, a fact Vic had discerned pretty damn quickly the night before. They'd been practically dry humping in Brantley's Jock Stock Room, the trophy room housing memorabilia from all his superstar clients.

And wasn't it a sorry statement on Vic's life that he was more interested in seeing if Brantley had kept any of his stuff—his jersey, maybe, or his rookie card—in the famed arsenal than watching Lara Wyland trying to squirm her way out of her clothes?

How the mighty had freaking fallen.

Judging from the long looks Brantley and the chick were giving each other now, Vic would have a chance to watch the replay of the sweaty sex he'd missed out on the night before. But right now he needed to check his preparations for a few surprises he had in store this weekend.

He wouldn't be caught off guard now that he had maneuvered Brantley to the most remote property that guy owned. Vic had a safety net here, a little place of his own on the St. Lawrence that would come in handy for a final showdown.

Of course, Lara's presence made things more interesting. She would make Dex more vulnerable. And they were both so caught up in each other that they didn't seem to have a clue what was going on all around them. Some psychic Lara had turned out to be.

Anger bubbled all over again at the knowledge they'd railroaded him together—ganging up on him to make him think he was losing his freaking mind. Rage clouded his vision and threatened to swamp him with too much emotion to carry out his well-laid plans. With an effort, he pushed it all back and stamped it down, boxing it up into a far corner of his mind to deal with another day. First he needed to find the ideal time to strike. To divide and conquer.

The only question was, should he take Lara? Or stick with his original plan and grab Dex?

No doubt the psychic would be easier. And assuming Dex was as hot for her as it looked from Vic's vantage point, Lara's distress would bring the main target anyhow.

More trouble was brewing in the formerly perfect world of Dexter Brantley; he just didn't know it yet.

It wouldn't be a quick and painless end for Dex the Hex since the guy had never let anyone else end a career in a painless way. Vic enjoyed the slow build to the drama as much as he anticipated the finale.

Dexter Brantley was about to find out just how cursed a man could be.

"WHAT WAS THAT?"

Lara straightened, her hand clutching Dex's arm in a grip that surprised him. She stared up at the roof.

Had she heard something or had all the talk of a possible trespasser put them both on edge? He stilled. Listened.

He owed her that much after he'd given her a hard time about listening to ghosts. She didn't deserve the hassle since he'd been the one to hire her. It wasn't her fault he had big-time mixed feelings on the whole psychic thing.

"I don't hear anything except the rain. It's turning to sleet now, that's why there's so much noise."

Her hand lingered on his arm, frozen in its grip as she

waited, listening. That simple touch turned him inside out with no effort on her part. He wanted to guide her hand off his arm and down to his thigh.

But the house telephone rang just then and in light of all the chaos around him lately, he decided he'd better sprint for it.

Damn it.

Service could easily cut out in this kind of weather and with his business falling deeper and deeper in the red, he needed to talk to at least a half a dozen people as soon as possible.

The business of a sports agent wasn't all negotiating contracts and endorsement deals. Ninety percent of his work involved hand-holding and playing psychologist on the fly. A young QB worried about his future prospects when his shoulder hurt—that meant an hour on the phone reassuring him he'd be fine. An Eastern European skater worried about how to care for her sick mother overseas until she cut a big deal—that meant helping her find a cheap maid or live-in helper for her mom.

Dex couldn't even think about turning off a phone or he could lose a prime client to another agent who would be there when their athletes needed something. Anything.

So with the NFL draft looming and his rookies getting more and more wound up, Dex needed to speak with Massimo—among others—today.

"Sorry, Lara. Hold that thought, okay?"

Retrieving the phone from a far corner of the large library, Dex settled into a chair behind the old-fashioned cherry desk. Still frustrated with the lack of answers about who might be trying to sabotage his whole life, he wondered how to best utilize Lara's remaining time here this weekend.

Since his bigger motive for having her up here wouldn't come together until Sunday at the earliest, he wished they could just spend the rest of their time in bed and forget all about trespassers—ghostly and otherwise. The cops could take care of the real ones and his upcoming media campaign could spin away the curse. He refused to care about the thwarted love affair of a long-dead relative.

"Hello?"

A sharp burst of static greeted him before he discerned a voice.

"…accelerant at the scene. We're talking to the Manhattan fire officials on Monday to coordinate efforts."

"Is this about the Aspen fire?" Dex leaned forward in his chair. "Who did you say you were? We've got some weather up here and the connection is poor."

More static cracked through the line. He thought he heard something about a fire marshal's office, but then the line went out again as a gust of wind rocked the high windowpanes. The connection went silent.

"Damn it."

"Is everything okay?" Lara's voice broke in on his thoughts a moment before she peered around a bookshelf.

"I guess so." How did one react to the news that one's house—no, two houses—had been purposely set aflame? "The connection went dead, but I'm pretty sure that was the fire marshal in Aspen. He said something about an accelerant being used and getting in touch with the New York arson investigator next week."

"News which supports your sabotage theory." She still

held the red family history book, her one finger sand-
wiched between pages to keep her place.

A reminder she wouldn't let go of her own theories.

"News which should tell you that you don't need to
worry about whatever a bunch of my cranky ancestors are
saying." He stared up at her in the dim lights of the library,
wishing she would start having sexually oriented visions
again. They were a hell of a lot more fun than images of
century-old crackpots.

"You know what it was like to listen to a phone conversation through the interference of a storm?" She
straightened, hugging the book to her chest as a blast of
sleet pelted the windows overhead.

He nodded, not sure where she was going with this.

"That's what it's like for me trying to tune into the
regular world when my psychic senses are active and responding to strong stimuli. It doesn't matter how much
I strain to hear through the interference, I just can't pick
up the frequency of regular life." She shrugged, displac-
ing the shoulder of her wide-necked purple sweater. "I'm
better off working with the psychic disruptions and
trying to smooth them over because the more I tune
them out, the stronger they become. If I ignore it long
enough, my whole electromagnetic field goes out of
whack and I start stopping clocks and setting off alarms
wherever I go."

Her words brought home how obnoxious he'd been to
her ever since she'd left his bed at the crack of dawn.

"Well you can't make the electromagnetic field any
worse in this house since we have a long history of clocks
stopping and the power going out." He pulled an ottoman

forward and waved her toward it. "Is there anything I can do to help you do your job?"

"I'd like to spend some time reading before the lights go off." They flickered again in an ominous blackout. "I know you don't want to believe that I was purposely drawn to this book on shelves full of thousands, but my guess is that there is something compelling in here, something I need to understand in order to help you."

His eyes lingered on the skin bared by her slipping sweater. The urge to follow the shape of her collarbone with his tongue was strong.

But he needed to listen. Pay attention. She was hell-bent on reading about his family's history, so he nodded, doing his best to seem reassuring and nonjudgmental. Dex knew that if he ever wanted another chance to touch Lara, he would have to remain open to her work and her beliefs about the world.

He couldn't just pay lip service to ghosts and visions. He needed to give her room to work without attempting to seduce her. The notion sucked even as he knew it was the right thing to do.

"Okay. You want to learn more about the family history even though the curse seems more and more implausible. Fair enough." He drummed his fingers idly on his knees trying to understand her better the same way he would try to get a fix on a new client. "Because you need to use these—ah—senses to keep them sharp, right?"

"Yes." Her fingers smoothed over her shoulder before gripping the neckline of her sweater and tugging it back into place. "And also because I'm trying to shed some light on the dark aura that seems to be hanging over the house and maybe over you, too. If we address that, we might ease some of the smaller problems like the blight in the chef's herbs and the kitchen accidents."

Still mourning the loss of his visual on her exposed shoulder, Dex couldn't stop himself from reaching out to touch her there. He would leave her alone and respect her work—soon. He needed this small reward for his restraint first, however.

"Is there anything I can do to help?"

He kept his touch light and—he hoped—unaggressive. This woman did have a knack for sensing emotions.

"I'd rather read on my own, but if you want to work on that list of enemies, I think it would help the police when you report the incident with your boat, and it will definitely help the arson investigators when they move forward."

She hadn't shaken off his touch, hadn't reminded him that she wanted him to respect her boundaries, but he could almost see it in her eyes. She was about to say something.

How could he forestall her objections?

In negotiations for his clients, he usually returned to his talking points before a team could shoot down his contract terms. When Dex felt a team's management balking at what he asked, he hyped up his client's worth verbally, spelling out what exactly made the athlete such a hot commodity.

In this case, it was Lara who was ready to balk and it was Dex who needed to be hyped. He couldn't think of any way to talk himself up, however, so he decided to show her exactly what she'd be missing out on if she pulled away from him.

Leaning forward, he brushed his lips over the place

where her neck met her shoulder. Her soft, sweet fragrance wafted up from her skin, filling his nostrils and reminding him of the night they'd shared. Moments when their limbs had been entwined, moments when his hips had moved against hers with slow deliberation.

The memories rolled over him in sweetly painstaking detail. He dipped his tongue into the hollow at the base of her throat. Her heartbeat tripped along at high speed, her pulse pumping overtime beneath his mouth.

He wanted to continue, his whole body primed and ready for a repeat of the night before, but he knew he needed to let her go. She would resent being maneuvered if he didn't back off.

With regret, he broke off the kiss and retreated to his seat. Lara's eyes were dazed, her breathing accelerated.

Clearing his throat, Dex stood.

"Then I'll let you get to your reading." He needed to put his feet in motion now or he'd never leave. "But I have to admit I hope you'll be thinking about me more than a bunch of dead people. I'll be in the room across the hall if you need me when the lights go out."

Turning on his heel, he started for the exit, his whole body rigid from holding himself back. He didn't know if she would come to him this afternoon, but he damn well knew he had to let her make the next move.

7

___

"WAIT A MINUTE." Lara stood, tension coiled tight inside her as she set the family history book aside.

Dex turned to face her, not even having the good grace to look guilty for purposely trying to rev her hormones when she'd asked him very nicely to please give her some space.

"Yes?" His gray eyes weren't exactly cool and detached, but he didn't appear ready to crawl out of his skin the way she felt right now.

"Care to tell me what that was all about?" She crossed the library to meet him in the middle of the room. The storm raged all the louder over their heads where the sleet ping, ping, pinged at the dome of leaded glass.

"I don't know what you mean." His gaze remained unblinking, lending him a facade of detached objectivity while she swore someone had tied a knot inside her.

"What gives with the kiss even though I specifically requested a little breathing room to pull my head together after last night?" Desire flowed through her veins, thick and hot until she could almost swear the sleet must be steaming off the glass overhead.

She couldn't tell if her reaction to him was a case of pure passion and attraction, or if his kiss had spurred the same kind of psychic sexual energy that had driven her into his bed last night.

Or if—dear God in heaven—she currently suffered from both of those things.

"I've been holding back all day." He stroked a stray strand of hair from her cheek, even that gentle touch acting on her body like a potent drug.

"We've only been abstaining for—" she glanced at the looming grandfather clock in the corner "—eight hours and seventeen minutes." She meant to push his hand away, to reassert herself before she wound up naked and writhing on one of the library's leather-covered benches.

The ticktock of the clock's pendulum echoed the pounding of her heart.

"Yeah? Felt more like a lifetime to me." His voice slid over her senses, soothing the rough places—the spots that had been edgy and restless all morning since she hadn't even given herself the chance to wake up in his arms.

She'd run at the first sign of trouble, a stunt she'd perfected over the span of a very short and uneventful dating life.

"Lara?" His fingers drifted from the stray hair to her cheek, his thumb tracing a line down to her jaw.

Only then did she realize what a hypocrite she was being to demand space and then welcome his touch so easily. She tried to back up, but his arm snaked around her waist, holding her in place. There could be no missing his attraction to her now.

"What?" The rush of her heartbeat echoed in her ears, making it difficult to hear.

"Why deny what we both want so much?" His thumb dipped to her mouth, skimming a touch across the surface of her lower lip while another gust of wind rattled the windows. A tree limb cracked somewhere outside with an awful, shuddering creak.

Dex's molten brown gaze never left hers.

"I told you earlier." Her voice seemed to have been half strangled out of her, perhaps because she wanted nothing more than to arch up on her toes and kiss him. Nip his bottom lip curled into an arrogant smile. Draw that tender bit of flesh into her mouth until he couldn't help but kiss her in return. "I can't be with someone who doesn't respect what I do."

"Can't I question the nature of the supernatural while still respecting your work?" The motion of his touch, the rhythmic slide of his thumb from one side of her mouth to the other, seemed to have her hypnotized. "Isn't it common in your business for people to be interested in your methods even if they totally buy into psychic phenomenon? People are drawn to your work because it's alternative and not scientific. When rational explanations fail, your clients want to explore those alternatives. That nonscientific nature is exactly what makes people so curious about your skills, right?"

She could see his point. Her work was interesting because it was unusual and she should be prepared for people who wanted to understand it better.

Then again, she might just be swayed by the fact that Dex stood so close to her while the world seemed to be coming apart outside the safe haven of the library.

In answer, she merely nipped at his thumb, drawing it in between her teeth to suck lightly. Her eyes fell closed as she allowed herself this small pleasure, her other senses heightening to take in the aroma of him. She'd hated show-ering this morning because it had meant washing off his scent and now she wanted it all over her with a feral longing she'd never felt toward another man.

Whatever restraints Dex had put on himself to hold back from her today, he loosened them now. His grip tightened on her waist, his fingers flexing in the soft silk and mohair sweater, the heat of his palm permeating her clothes.

"Can I take this to mean I'm forgiven for doubting your methods?" He whispered into her ear while he moved his hand up her back, methodically pressing each new square inch of her closer to him.

Releasing his thumb, she licked her lips, surprised how erotic that simple act felt.

"Depends." Lara felt dizzy from the onslaught of sen-sations, her knees threatening to give out at any second as her gaze met his again. "How fast do you think you can be naked and ready for me?"

"I've been ready since I rolled out of bed this morning and I can be naked in about 1.3 seconds." He pulled her sweater down her shoulder to expose her where he'd kissed her earlier.

She shivered as his eyes raked over her, taking in every last detail.

"Then the answer is yes. You are forgiven, contingent upon stripping to my satisfaction." She tunneled her hands up and under his shirt, hungry for the feel of skin-on-skin contact. "Fast, I mean. I don't need anything artful, I just need fast."

Surprise registered on his face for only a moment before his expression turned hot. Intense.

He lifted his arms to pluck the shirt up and off, his sculpted body the stuff women's fantasies were made of. She couldn't wait to roam her fingers—her tongue—over every last inch of him.

"Lara." He reached for his belt while she leaned in to kiss his chest. "What did I ever do to make you think I wouldn't hold up my end of a bargain?"

He unzipped and half a second later he seemed to be stepping out of his pants and his shoes, too. And oh. My. Stars.

This was a fine male specimen.

Her whole body started to tremble in sweet anticipation. The gorgeous muscles in his arms hadn't elicited the kind of orgasmic fever in her that the taut sinews of his thighs produced. He might as well have tattooed All Night Long on his hip, because that was the message sent out by the rock-solid strength of his lower body.

"Yes." A thousand times yes. "I believe you can deliver whatever I ask for tonight."

She had been so caught up in half-baked visions and sexual images the night before that she hadn't been able to really appreciate the reality of who was in her bed and what he had to offer. She could see that—and him—now, however.

"What about you?" He backed her toward one of the benches ringing the room, his bare legs brushing up against hers. "Would you like some help undressing?"

"Yes." She needed help with everything because her world seemed to be coming apart at the seams ever since she'd entered this house. She'd never been so gripped by powerful forces as during her time under Dex's roof—his curse and despair, the house's long history of lost love, her own inexplicable reaction to a client whose stance on psychic phenomenon was dismissive at best. They all conspired to keep her attention focused on the man at the center of all that turmoil.

He skimmed her sweater up and off as they reached one of the wide, leather-covered benches scattered around the room. Light from the leaded glass dome above splashed down on them.

"Better?"

She nodded, her voice as muddled as her thoughts, and let the heat between them dictate what would happen. Whether it was wise to be with Dex again or not, she couldn't deny the sense of inevitability that took over when he was around.

Now, his hands ducked beneath her bra straps and smoothed a path down her tender flesh to the swell of her breasts. The storm outside echoed the one inside her, the sleet keeping pace with her heartbeat. The wind beating on the house seemed as relentless as her hunger for Dex, the power of it too strong to ignore.

He unfastened her bra, freeing her aching breasts. She wanted more from him, faster. His nakedness made her impatient. But he seemed content to watch her, to study her as she fell helpless into the abyss of desire all over again.

Her thigh brushed his leg and her belly nudged his thick erection. His eyes rolled back for just a moment, clouding at that contact.

And that was all she needed to know, all the reassurance she could ask for that this deluge of sexual need wasn't one-sided. She wrapped her hand around the engorged shaft, her fingers tracing the path of the wide vein up the front of him.

A shudder passed over him and she dropped to her knees, possessed with the desire to taste him. To make him lose any hint of cool reserve and join her in the conflagration of senses.

She would make him feel what she felt, make him see the world through emotional eyes, if only for a little while.

Dex's thoughts turned to gibberish, his plan for seduction reduced to ashes at the first stroke of Lara's pink tongue.

He didn't know how he'd scavenge any restraint when seeing her half-naked body perched between his thighs was enough to make a man forget his own name. But closing his eyes tormented him even more since then his only option was to concentrate on the undiluted sensation of her soft lips and tongue bringing him closer and closer to an incredible brink—

"Lara." Her name was a plea for mercy, his muscles so taut he could scarcely move. "Sweetheart, you need to—"

He really almost didn't make it, but she paused just then to peer up at him and see what he wanted. That reprieve alone saved him. He hauled her to her feet while he still could, peeling off her skirt and panties with all possible haste.

"You don't want me to finish?" She licked her lips with slow deliberation as he sank down on the bench. The seating in the library had all been bolted into the floor like church pews, so it would be stable enough, even if there wouldn't be anything remotely holy taking place on these seats.

"You'll arrive at a great finish, I promise." He pulled her on top of him, and she fell into his lap, her body on full display. Her limbs were surprisingly strong and slim, her movements graceful as she found a comfortable position.

"You're in way too good shape for a psychic." He drew his palm slowly up her toned calf, savoring the feel of her soft skin and the subtle scent of spring flowers around her.

"You wound me yet again with your assumptions, Mr. Brantley." Thankfully, she didn't appear terribly upset as she wrapped her arms around his neck and arched her back to rub her breasts against his chest. "As a psychic, I make time in my schedule to align my chakras on a regular basis with yoga."

"I should have guessed." He pressed his mouth to hers, needing a taste. She was so different from any woman he'd ever dated, so interested in the world beyond herself. Most of his clients had to be very performance oriented and—like it or not—extremely focused on their bodies as tools for achieving their potential.

But Lara just happened to get great physical benefits because she worked hard to obtain a mental benefit. He admired that about her. In her own way, she was as dedicated to her craft as any top-notch professional athlete.

Her fingers threaded through his hair as she leveraged herself up higher against him. He palmed a breast, taking the weight of her soft flesh in his hand. With slow deliberation he dragged a thumb over the taut peak. Her breath snagged in her throat, her fingers tightening on his shoulders.

He broke the kiss to meet her gaze and she dragged her

eyes open with an effort, her long lashes fanning her cheeks. Air heaved in and out of his lungs, his chest rising and falling with the powerful effect of kissing her. Her mouth was swollen from his attention, her soft lips damp and pink.

"Can you read my mind now?" He didn't try to shock her with his thoughts the way he had yesterday, but he did allow himself to envision her naked and drenched with water, her beautiful body glistening with rivulets of water he licked off her one by one....

She shook her head, the dark mass of her hair sliding over her shoulders.

"No. I tend to read people better when I first meet them." Her hands trembled lightly against his shoulders. "Plus I see less when I'm wrapped up in a moment. Like now."

She shifted in his lap, her bare hip rocking with a swivel that robbed him of words for a long moment.

"Why do you ask?" she prodded, untwining an arm from around his neck to graze her fingertips down his chest to his waist. His abs.

Hell. Hanging on to a thought was like cupping water in his bare hands. Reason leaked away with every sigh and shift of her gorgeous body.

"I just want to know any time that you are in my head with me, okay?" The notion of that kind of connection still made him uneasy; a hypocritical thought, perhaps, when they were about to connect physically as close as two people could get.

She nodded as if understanding, her hand pausing in its downward trek for a moment before her fingers whispered along the ridge of his shaft.

Outside the rain and sleet had quieted. He suspected it

had turned to snow. The light filtering in grew darker, leaving him wrapped in shades of gray with Lara's tempting touches and his own hunger for more.

The scent of her arousal drove his higher. She hummed low in her throat as he transferred his palms to her thighs. The appeal of that sound was earthy and immediate, a mating call only he could respond to.

The hum nudged up an octave as he neared the juncture of her thighs, her muscles flexing and tightening. Her whole body strained toward him, her back arching, breasts lifting.

He took one pink bud in his mouth, sucking lightly, rolling the tip between his teeth until she twisted in his arms, offering up the other breast for feasting.

He complied gladly, never ceasing his slow trek up her inner thigh to the source of her heat. She shuddered on contact, his finger just barely sketching along the swollen seam between her legs. She was wet and ready for him, her juices so slick on his finger he brought one digit to his mouth for a taste.

Whimpering, she scooted back on his lap to his knees until she had enough room to straddle him. She rocked her hips against his, creating a friction so sweet he could have climaxed right then and there.

"Wait." He reached for protection, knowing he had put a condom somewhere on the bench.

She found it before he did and tore the packet open with her teeth. He steeled himself for the feel of her hands on him before she rolled the prophylactic in place.

Patience. Damn it, but he needed some now. He cupped her bottom and lifted her up, positioning her above him. Then, forcing himself to drag in a few steadying breaths, he entered her in one long, slow slide, thrusting upward as she locked her legs around his waist.

He held himself there, feeling their hearts beat in sync, inside and out. The sound mesmerized him as it reverberated through them both at the same time. He watched her, unblinking, as they connected on a level they hadn't breached the night before. This wasn't a frenzy of sex to ease a wild craving. This was something deeper and more powerful. A joining.

Lara stroked his face and squeezed her inner muscles, silent demands he met with pleasure. He kissed her as he levered her up again, just enough to create the sweet friction they both wanted.

Heat seared him. Sweat broke out along his forehead as he set up a deliberate, aching rhythm. Every withdrawal ended in a rejoining so sweet Lara cried out with every thrust.

He sensed the end coming closer and struggled to hang on, to savor every delectable inch of her while he had her wrapped all around him. He ran his hands over the silky skin of her thighs and up her spine. Tipping her backward, he kissed her breasts, teasing the nipples into the tightest possible buds.

Her heels dug into his back, her body going taut and he knew she was moments away from her peak. He pressed his thumb between her legs, massaging her softly until spasms rolled through her, her whole body tensing with completion.

Everything inside him stilled, absorbing the lush contractions of her sex around him and the power of what was happening between them. Then the tide became too strong to hold back and he went under, losing himself in the moment and *her.*

Vaguely, he was aware of her hands stroking over his chest, her mouth raining damp kisses all over his face and shoulders. His shout drowned out her rasping breaths for a moment, making him deaf to anything but his own pleasure.

It took a moment, then, for him to comprehend Lara's openmouthed scream.

He froze, uncomprehending, as she shoved him down to his back and the sky fell in above them. Shards of leaded glass from the domed ceiling shattered beside them. Sleet and snow swirled into the room, raining over the books and icing their heated skin.

8

LARA SHIVERED under a blanket in the guest bedroom while Dexter finished securing the gaping hole in the roof of the library. The glass hadn't covered a huge space—only about six feet—but it had seemed like more when it had cracked beneath the weight of the wet snow and sleet.

She'd offered to help Dex nail up some boards over the area, but he'd refused on the grounds that he couldn't take the guilt if the curse hurt her any worse than it already had.

Rubbing her fingers over the bandage on her lower back where a chunk of glass had made the deepest scratch, Lara reached for the family history book she'd taken from the library after they'd cleaned up the room. She was eager to help Dex put this curse to rest, whether or not he fully believed in it. He'd seemed almost relieved to know someone was trying to sabotage him, as if that proved there was no century-old negative energy swirling around his life.

Maybe studying the family's past would help. Smoothing her hands over the worn leather binding for a moment, Lara sensed many hands had held the volume and studied it before her. She cracked open the huge book and the pages fell immediately to a photo of the man she'd seen on the staircase fighting with his mistress.

Dex's great-grandfather.

"Lara."

She started at the sound of her name whispered by an unfamiliar voice. A woman's voice.

After so many years of experience with paranormal phenomenon, Lara wished she wasn't still so unsettled by the presence of spirits. Tightening the blanket around her shoulders, she peered about the room for signs of any stray energy.

"Yes?" Her own voice came out in a disconcerted rasp, her whole body rebelling the fast-forward changes in her world today after going from the most sublime sex imaginable to abject fear at falling glass and now—this?

"The Brantley men are scoundrels." The voice gained strength, sounding indignant and impossibly well-bred, like a *New Yorker* caricature come to life.

"Who are you?" She spoke aloud even though there were schools of thought that suggested conversations with the dead could be carried out mentally.

Lara remained of the opinion that conversing out loud clarified the discussion and kept her focused. Besides, this wasn't her area of expertise. Chatting with dead people unnerved her. Especially when she could not see them.

"I am a woman scorned. A mistress tossed aside like a bit of old rubbish." A whisper of cold air blew past Lara's cheek even though no window had been opened.

She held her shiver in check, recognizing the sign of a full-fledged ghost. She hadn't wanted to use the word with Dex who seemed to carry such a healthy dose of cynicism about her work anyway. But whatever Lara chatted with now, it wasn't a mere psychic impression. Tightening her hold on the bedspread, she appreciated the way the feel of the material world kept her grounded.

"I'm sorry." Lara sensed the spirit's despair, a pang that resonated deeply within her own heart. "I've felt that way before."

A shape materialized slowly by the wall of plum-colored drapes covering the windows. The figure was a mist of gray light that formed into an old-fashioned dress with a tiny waist, then a bodice of endless ruffles, and finally a heart-shaped feminine face.

It was the same woman she'd seen falling down the stairs earlier in the day.

"You've known the touch of a Brantley man then." The woman stared at her with such knowing certainty, Lara couldn't stop the moment of fear that perhaps Dex would break her heart.

Only if she were so foolish as to get that precious piece of her involved.

"It was another man who played me." She felt some of the day's icy sleet around her heart at the memory.

"But at least you did not die the same day you discovered the truth." The misty shape wavered slightly. "There was no time to come to terms with the betrayal *I* faced, and I died in a moment of utter devastation and fury."

Lara's mind flashed back to the quarrel she'd witnessed, followed by that ungodly fall….

"Lara." From outside the door, Dex knocked.

The woman dissipated, fading as quickly as she had formed while Lara tried to forestall her.

"Wait. Are you saying he killed you? You died when you fell down those stairs?" Surely that hadn't been part of the history as Dex understood it or he would have mentioned it.

"Lara?" Dex called again, louder this time, while the voice of the apparition remained silent.

"Come in." Lara slid her legs off the bed to stand, still clutching the blanket around her shoulders. She'd saved her skirt from the wreckage of the library, but her purple sweater had been saturated with wet snow so she wore one of Dex's shirts. A batting jersey, he'd said, from one of his college clients turned pro.

The University of Florida colors clashed mightily with her violet skirt, but she was just glad to be warm again.

The door creaked open and Dex stepped inside. He had a bandage above his left eye, one she'd placed there to stop the bleeding of a cut from a pane he'd been moving.

"Everything okay in here?" He glanced around the fresco-covered room, eyes narrowed.

No doubt he'd heard her talking to someone else.

"Fine. I was just communing with—some of the house's energy forces."

He paused in his trek toward her for a moment before regaining his momentum, damp droplets dotting his long wool coat.

"Is that different from the impressions you saw earlier?"

She had to smile at his cautious use of her lingo as he slid off his coat and tossed it on a chest at the end of the bed.

"For me personally, yes. Some psychics experience different phenomenon to varying degrees depending where their skills lie. My sense of presence with the energy field that was here a moment ago was much stronger than this morning on the stairwell." She didn't want to overload him with psychobabble, but he seemed to need the extra information to accept her process. "As it happened, the presence I was just speaking with was your great-grand-father's mistress, the same woman I saw fall down the stairs earlier."

He sat down on the four-poster bed, his expression a bit dazed.

"You were talking to…a ghost?"

Unable to resist, she swiped a hand across his head to brush away some of the icy dampness from his skin.

"I prefer not to think in those terms because the word has too many connotations of cartoonish spirits whisking around the planet in long white sheets." She sat beside him, the edge of her blanket spilling onto his knee. "Every old house has some kind of spirit history, a connection to those who've lived there before. It's the reason places like a historic battlefield inspire such a somber feeling of quiet reverence even centuries after the battles are over."

Dex nodded and didn't argue, whether or not he believed her.

"So did the woman confess to making my world a living hell lately?" He ran a hand over the book she'd been reading before he stroked a caress down her arm.

Shivering in the wake of that touch, Lara mourned the fact that they hadn't been able to sleep in each other's arms or at least talk about what had happened between them af-terward. They'd been too busy scrambling to clean up before more snow got in the roof.

"She faded before I had the chance to ask." Lara took a deep breath, thinking the best way to share her next bit of news was all at once. "But for what it's worth I don't think she knows anything about a curse, because she said she died after that fall."

A COOL DRAFT seemed to penetrate the windows of the guest room.

Dex's skin chilled, his brain struggling to adapt to Lara's world. He'd messed up a conversation with her about this stuff earlier. He wouldn't screw things up again.

"The woman who supposedly cursed my great-grand-father—my whole family—just up and died?" He tried to navigate the implications of that news. "Are you saying she died without uttering the curse? That the family stories about her all these years were false?"

His granddad had passed along the tale himself as he'd heard it from his mother. But maybe she'd spun the story for the benefit of her son, covering up an accident that might have been—murder?

"I didn't have the chance to speak to her for long." She relayed the words spoken by the "energy force" that sure as hell sounded like a ghost to him.

"She sounds like she was bitter enough to have cursed him." Not that Dex understood how a few words spoken in anger before he was born could account for the rash of bad luck that had smothered his life for the last year.

He stared up at one of the frescoes on the walls of the guest suite—depicting a turn-of-the-century boat race around Brantley Island—and wondered if the woman in question had been painted into any of the old scenes from life on the river. Was the face of the infamous mistress here somewhere without him knowing?

"I'm sure she was bitter. But the fact that the family legend and the reality *might* have been different doesn't necessarily change the end result. Even if she didn't speak a curse, she might have carried that ill will with her into death." Lara tugged the blue fleece blanket closer around her shoulders, her face pale and her hair pinned up with a few damp pieces around her neck as if she'd taken a bath. "The sentiments of those who have passed beyond the veil can have a powerful effect on the living."

"Great-granddad's mistress is still so pissed three—or is it four?—generations later that she decided to make my life miserable once I turned thirty-three?"

It wasn't that he *didn't* believe, per se. But how could a dead woman be so vindictive?

Lara shrugged, one shoulder easing out of the blanket with the gesture. She wore a jersey that belonged to him underneath, a fact that sent a stab of possessiveness through him. He'd been so damn scared for her when that domed roof had caved in. Seeing blood on her back had damn near taken years off his life.

"Not necessarily. I'd like to wander around the house more today and get a feel for the energy at work, but my first inclination is that uneasy spirits might account for the problems around this property. However, I highly doubt that kind of energy would have any effect on you when you're away from this island."

Pulling the blanket back over her shoulder, she tucked her feet beneath her on the bed. His brief glimpse of her bare toes reminded him of her vulnerability here.

He reached out to stroke her hair, the dark mass tilting to one side in its haphazard pile on her head.

"I just don't want you to do anything that might stir up…negative energy." He didn't like the idea of her communicating with some crazy, pissed-off ghost in here alone. "I don't want anything to happen to you because of me."

"Trust me, I know how to protect myself against that kind of thing." Something in her tone told him this would be a prickly subject to get into with her.

He trailed his hand down her cheek, cradling her jaw.

"I'm sure you do, but that roof caving in was no small act of mischief. You could have been seriously injured."

Or worse. The thought knotted in a cold ball at the pit of his stomach. He brushed her hair away from her temple, all of her so soft. Fragile. He half wished he hadn't asked her to come, hadn't put her in this kind of danger. But then he would have missed getting to be with her, getting to know her.

"That's why I think you need police assistance in addition to my help. I know I perceived a mental image of an angry man cutting that rope on your stolen boat. When the cops come to check that out, they can look for evidence around the roof to see if someone tampered with the dome."

He'd already been outside to check for himself, but the wet snow piling up covered any footprints that might have been around the library. He released her, sensing she still balked at the idea of mixing business and pleasure.

Sensed?

Maybe Lara was having more of an effect on him than he realized if he was beginning to mysteriously perceive things around him instead of seeing, hearing or otherwise using his five concrete senses.

"I didn't see any signs of a strange boat around the island earlier, but someone could have tinkered with the roof weeks ago." The island didn't have any major security systems other than a generic alarm on the house that would be tripped by entrance through a door or window.

After this weekend, Dex planned to install video cameras around the island to monitor uninvited boat traffic and anything else out of the ordinary on this isolated piece of property. Losing his other homes to fire had been scary and inconvenient. Losing this place to someone's malevolence would be unthinkable.

"So what do you think we should do until the storm dies down and the police can come?" She picked at the satin binding on the blanket, her fingers restless. Nervous?

"Hmm…isolated on a remote island with a sexy psychic for the night? I'm sure I can come up with something." He brushed a kiss over her full lips, remembering the ways she'd used her pretty mouth to drive him wild.

Just then, the lights went out. The whole house took on an eerie silence broken only by the rush of wind against the old walls and a startled gasp from Lara's lips.

"No power," Lara whispered, easing back from him in the darkness. "Do you think we lost it naturally or—could someone have cut it on purpose?"

Any hope he had of laying Lara back onto the bed for the rest of the evening vanished. His muscles tensed, his mind racing ahead to where he'd find a flashlight even though he didn't want to leave her alone.

Unprotected.

"What do your psychic senses say? Can you feel out

stuff like that?" He covered her hand with his, listening intently for any strange noises in the house.

Her breath sounded shaky as she inhaled. Exhaled. Then finally spoke.

"There is a lot of unusual energy throughout the property to begin with, but I don't feel the presence of anyone new." Frowning, she peered up at him. "I just worry if—what if someone's been on the island ever since I arrived? I *did* pick up a sense of ill will humming in the air then and I don't think it came from an angry chef."

They remained still, breathing each other's air, caution outweighing desire. He didn't think he could have overlooked a stranger on the island, but then again, he hadn't visited all the outbuildings on the property after arriving. He didn't think he should do that now and leave Lara alone, but he would have to at least look into the power outage and make sure the main house was secure.

"I'd better go check the fuse box and power source." He'd far rather wrap Lara around him all night long, but his unlucky streak continued. "I'll lock the door behind me. When I come back, I'll bring some candles and a flashlight for you."

Lara watched him leave the guest room, waiting for him to close the door behind him before she resorted to total panic.

He'd asked her to use her psychic abilities—abilities he struggled to believe in the first place—and she'd come up frighteningly blank. Her skill was softening by the hour, less sharp tonight than it had been even this morning.

And there could be only one explanation.

"Damn it." She tossed aside the blanket she'd been

wearing like a shawl and hopped off the bed to take up a yoga position on the floor.

If ever a woman needed to meditate, the time was now. Lara's feelings were mixed-up, her emotions drawn to a man she'd been determined not to like. A man she never should have slept with because of her relationship with him as a client. And now her psychic field had diminished in proportion to her feelings for him, the way it had the one other time in her life when she'd allowed herself to care about a man.

Taking a deep breath, she tried to clear the monkey chatter of her thoughts, wishing she could forget that caring about someone made her less intuitive about their needs. Their thoughts. It made it harder to lie to herself.

If she'd just *slept* with Dex, they wouldn't have a problem. The complications arose when her heart got involved. And now—like it or not—her sudden psychic blind spot where he was concerned would have a huge negative impact on her work here.

"Ohm." She breathed the word on an exhale, feeling the vibration of the sound up the back of her throat and resonating through her skull.

The low, resonant humming normally centered her, but today, she feared her efforts were akin to turning up the radio loud when a friend was saying something you didn't want to hear. No matter how Lara attempted to drown out the frantic messages from her subconscious, they came through anyway.

"Ohmmmm."

The sound that should be drawing her deeper into mental peace and serenity acted like a drugstore brand bandage on a gaping wound. Her efforts to staunch the flow of gut-gnawing worries were useless.

Giving up, she lay back on the floor. She'd messed up this job so badly. She might have put Dex in greater danger by giving him a false sense of security that she would intuit the arrival of danger on his doorstep.

And damn it, after this move—having sex with the boss and possibly ruining any chance she'd be able to use her powers to help him—maybe she really was as grossly unprofessional as her mother's friends had accused her of being.

9

THE MATCH BLEW OUT AGAIN.

Dex cursed the storm, the draft through the old stone basement and his total lack of any household organization that might have helped him find a flashlight instead of a book of matches to use in making his way around the house.

Great-granddad was a murderer.

The thought slid into his consciousness even though he refused to believe it. Lara had admitted her "source" for the story—the spirit of great-granddad's dead mistress—could be biased. Or lying to cause trouble.

But the idea of a murder in the family still plagued him as he attempted to locate the fuse box in the basement without killing himself. The walls were stone and the dirt floor was damp, creating a stale, earthy scent. Finally, stepping over a crate full of long-forgotten uniforms for the household staff, Dex spotted the fuse box in the glow of a match quickly burning his fingers.

Steeling himself to the pain, he yanked open the box and found everything in order. Just the way it should be. No one had tampered with the power here deliberately and there was no evidence of anyone else in the house.

Thank God. At least they weren't in any kind of imme-diate danger. There had been no footsteps around the house when he'd checked the roof, and no one had been near the power source for the property. Apparently the curse—and the cut rope in the boathouse—had just made him extra wary.

Winding his way back through the maze of obstacles in the cellar, Dex debated the notion of a curse hanging over his family based on a Brantley committing an evil deed. He could buy into that more than the idea of a curse uttered by a scorned woman. If the mistress had really died at his great-grandfather's hands, there might be some kind of cosmic karma at work making his life a living hell. Maybe he could solve the problem by doing charitable deeds? Committing Brantley wealth to something that would honor this woman's memory?

He found himself eager to discuss the idea with Lara.

And how wild was that?

He'd brought Lara up here with every intention of em-ploying her skills mostly for the sake of showmanship. He'd spread the word around the small Thousand Islands community that a renowned psychic was in residence at Brantley House, and he'd hoped to use that to help get a follow-up article in the local paper. With a report that his luck had changed or that the bad vibes from the old mansion had been driven out for good, he could repair his damaged reputation in the eyes of any superstitious clients.

Yet Lara had offered him so much more than he'd expected in regard to untwining the real reasons for his bad luck. More than that, she'd related to him on a level that was genuine. Grounded. An odd observation about a

woman in a profession that required a belief in the paranormal, but he stood by it.

Lara wasn't the kind of woman who would be impressed
by his bottom line or his future income potential—the deter-
mining factors that had drawn women in his past. He'd grown
so used to putting on the show of success for his clients' sake
that he appreciated the opportunity to just be himself.

Pausing at the top of the stairs, he felt around some
storeroom shelves for a candle to take to Lara's room. He
needed to illuminate her in more ways than one, since he
hadn't gotten around to sharing the full extent of his hopes
for her work here. She'd asked to meet with the local newspaper columnist without any prompting from him, but considering their growing relationship, he no longer felt
comfortable arranging that meeting without telling Lara his
original plan to capitalize on her reputation in a PR campaign.

Imagining how that conversation might go, Dex's
feet slowed on the way up to the second floor. Would
she be angry? He hadn't really considered the implications of keeping his real motives for hiring her to
himself, but then, things had escalated between them so
incredibly fast.

Hoping to smooth his approach to the topic with a little
time to think about it, he decided to speak to her right after
he tried getting in touch with his office again. After all, he
couldn't afford to let his top football prospect cool his
heels for too long. College athletes were notorious for
getting antsy and overanxious before the draft—their
parents even more so. Dex didn't need Massimo pulling
out on him at the last minute.

And damn it, all that was true enough and not a justification for stalling a conversation with Lara he didn't particularly want to have.

Setting the candles he'd lit on a side table, he pulled out his cell phone to check for service. There was enough to at least place a call and he dialed up Massimo, who'd apparently phoned Dex's cell six times in the last twenty-four hours. Did he have to play babysitter 24-7 to every one of these guys? Dex had gotten into the business at a time when he'd enjoyed that nonstop action, the chance to be everybody's best friend. But after twelve years, having his work with him all day, every day was getting old.

Was it a coincidence that his view of the job had been clarified this weekend after spending time with Lara? He might be grateful to delay seeing her this red-hot second, but by and large, he resented how many times his work—or just thinking about his work—had waylaid him when he'd wanted to be with her.

What did that say about his feelings for her?

The call rang twice before someone picked up.

"Hello? Brantley?"

"Yeah, kid, it's me. Listen, I've got a crap connection and a—"

"Brant, man, I don't care about that shit. I've got offers from six other agents waiting to—" The connection blanked out for a minute before kicking back in again. "—and I freaking need some answers if you want to do this thing."

Even without hearing half of what the kid was saying, Dex knew the routine, the same crap he'd heard from every other antsy prospect before the draft.

"I've told you that you'll make more on the endorsement deals if you wait until after the draft. A number two pick or number ten pick is going to snag more than a number twenty guy and you're going to be in that top ten."

The call must have gone out again because he could hear Massimo yelling something about the pressure he was under to break his deal with Dexter, as if he hadn't even heard half of what Dex had been saying.

Crap. Dex sighed so hard he blew out one of the candles. He thumbed the off button on the phone, unwilling to repeat the same thing he'd told this guy ten other times before.

The better deals came *after* draft day for the guys sure to be taken in the top ten or fifteen spots. Lining up something now out of impatience didn't make any sense, but Dex knew damn well the other agents were planting doubts in the kid's head in the hope of luring him away from Dex. The agents would gladly take the lower endorsement offer for the kid if it meant signing him.

"Dex?"

Lara's voice drifted down the hall. At least he hoped it was her and not the ghost of Brantley House coming for him.

"Yeah." He scooped up the candles and made his way up the hall in the dark, knowing he couldn't put off his discussion with Lara any longer. He needed to come clean with his plan for capitalizing on her visit.

He just hoped she didn't mind a little extra media spotlight on her talents. Luckily, she seemed very confident in her skills. He couldn't imagine why she would want to hide her efforts to chase down the old curse.

"I CAN'T DO THAT."

Lara didn't know how else to put it, but hopping on the

publicity wagon for Dexter's image clean-up campaign definitely didn't fall under the heading of good uses of her abilities. She switched her weight from one foot to the other in the guest suite where she'd waited nervously for him to return. She hadn't even had the chance to feel relief that the lights had gone out naturally before he had sprung this on her.

"What do you mean you *can't* do it?" Dex's frustration was apparent even in the candlelit room, his broad shadow as ominous as his voice while he paced across the polished hardwood floor near the wall of floor-length velvet drapes. "Can't or won't, Lara? It couldn't be any easier to just explain to this reporter that you're helping me banish the curse."

Frustration simmered inside her as she considered that he'd almost certainly kept quiet about this until now on purpose. Did that mean he was…using her?

"I'm pretty sure you're aware that's a naive attitude regarding anyone in the press." She would give him the benefit of the doubt. Explain to him why she couldn't do what he wanted. "I can't just make a simple statement like that and have it be of any use to you. There will be follow-up questions, discussion of my methods, probably a few backhanded insinuations about the validity of what I do, and then a very public response that will put me in the hot seat for weeks afterward."

And she was so tired of being there.

"Isn't that common in your line of work? You find a missing person and then the media hop all over it for a few days before the interest dies down?" He checked his phone screen obsessively, flicking the unit open enough that she spotted the glow of the screen before he slammed it closed again. He'd asked to borrow hers in the hope that his battery had just been low, but she hadn't been able to get a signal, either.

Obviously, he still didn't have service and she knew that was equally responsible for his irritable mood.

Or—damn it—she supposed so. With her intuitive powers dulled around him, she had nothing to rely on but the same old guessing method any woman had at her disposal.

"No, that's not common. First of all, a psychic's work on a missing persons case is rarely reported to ensure police aren't overwhelmed by concerned intuitives calling in contributions on future cases. Secondly, when the instances *are* reported, the public is very amenable to our methods then because we were successful on a job they view as noble and worthwhile. But when it comes to things like breaking curses or ghost hunting, or anything else that strays firmly into the paranormal, trust me, the media isn't forgiving."

Jamming his phone back into his shirt pocket, Dex gave a terse nod.

"You don't want to deal with the fallout if someone says your work is a hoax. I get it. But keep in mind how quickly people bought into the hoax in the first place." His footsteps echoed on the hardwood as his leather loafers headed her way. "Media coverage of this thing turned a few bumps in my career into my worst nightmare. Image is everything in my business, Lara. And this reporter stole mine with one story that got picked up by a national news wire."

The resentment in his eyes wasn't directed toward her.

She understood that as his hands slipped over her shoulders, impressing his will on her through his skillful touch.

"It became a self-fulfilling prophecy." She knew how that worked and believed in the power of positive thinking because of it. But it only stood to reason the principle could work in reverse, as well.

"Exactly. The clients who heard about the curse freaked. They didn't care whether the curse was real, they cared about my reputation and they fled like rats from a flood."

"But if that's the case, then why am *I* here this weekend and not a good publicist?" The answer started taking shape as soon as she voiced the question. An answer confirmed by Dex's hands vanishing from her shoulders, his expression guilty as hell.

Oh crap.

"Lara—"

"But I am the publicist in a way, aren't I? Or at least, that's what you hoped I would be at the end of the weekend. You thought I'd jump at the chance to advertise my business with a splashy feature article explaining how I'd broken the curse for good."

A fact she didn't appreciate one bit. How could he have concealed such a big, fat secret agenda? She'd had every reason not to trust him after the incident with the NFL kicker, but she'd been swayed by the promise of a hefty retainer—and the opportunity to use her skills in an in-your-face manner after the criticism from conservative psychics. She'd been so preoccupied by her own hidden motives, she'd totally missed Dex's.

"Most people appreciate a chance to showcase their

work in a positive light." Dex still didn't seem to comprehend what upset her in all this, his expression blank.

"Most people also like to be hired to do a job that falls under their advertised services, not because they will be a convenient corporate mouthpiece." She would have felt used even if she hadn't made the mistake of sleeping with him this weekend. But considering she'd been taken in emotionally as well as professionally, Lara was angry. And yeah, hurt. "In other words, you never really cared about what I had to offer you in regard to my abilities as a psychic. You hired me to trot me out in front of the newspapers and your clients so the world will believe you're curse-free."

He didn't deny it, of course, because he couldn't. Lara couldn't have felt more off-balance if he'd yanked the small Persian rug right out from under her feet.

"I didn't think it was too much to ask to issue a statement regarding your work." He reached out to touch her but she dodged his hand, unwilling to fall under that spell.

"What work?" That's the part that got her. Lara knew the timing of this would spur even more flack in the psi community for her tendency to take jobs some deemed a questionable use of a psychic's time. "You don't even believe there's anything for me to do here, do you? You hired me to quiet the people who do believe in a curse, but when it comes right down to it, you really don't buy into it yourself, do you?"

"I tried to be very honest with you about not being sure what to think." His voice had turned quiet. "You really won't reconsider this?"

She recalled the generous retainer fee he had given her

and wondered if, ethically, she could really refuse. Of course, she could always refund the whole check, an option that seemed most logical in light of her disappearing psychic faculty.

And damn it, now that she thought about it, she had a small shortcoming of her own to confess.

"Actually, there are a few things I should tell you before I answer that." Her scalp itched with too many unsolved problems and tangled emotions. Her extra senses sputtered with strange blips of activity, showing her visions of the furniture maker who had handcrafted the bed over a century ago, and when she touched a side table, she saw a teenage maid breaking a small blue vase that had once sat on it.

On top of that, she saw a guy driving a bread truck, his uniform's logo matching the brand on the side of his van. How the hell did that relate to anything? Was that the company who delivered bread to the house?

All the random images acted like a psychic taunt since she couldn't really use her skills the way she wanted to now.

"I'm listening." He dropped onto the chest at the end of the bed, his elbows propped on his knees. He'd obviously gotten the message not to touch her since he kept his hands to himself.

She felt his full and undivided attention, something she'd bet he didn't give away often in his world of nonstop phone calls and high-stakes competition. A nervous shiver trembled over her skin.

"I've lost my psychic abilities where you're concerned." She folded her arms across her chest and waited for his reaction.

It seemed a long time coming. He stared at her without comment, his dark eyebrows scrunching hard before they lifted in surprise.

"I don't get it." Shrugging, he studied her in the candlelight, his eyes raking over her as if looking for clues to this change she'd mentioned.

"Sometimes when I grow close to someone, my abilities soften where they are concerned, almost as if nature is ensuring I don't have an advantage over the people in my life." The moment felt as intimate as any he'd been deep inside her, the words a confession that she felt something for him.

But would he recognize the significance of that admission, or would he simply be irritated that she couldn't follow through on the job? Then again, maybe he'd just see it as a cop-out, an excuse for not having the psychic abilities he'd never really believed she possessed in the first place?

"You can't tell what I'm thinking?"

"No, but that was never one of my claims—"

He lowered his voice. "You can't read my sexual thoughts anymore?"

Memories of some of his more graphic visions popped into her head, but they were just that—delicious memories from a titillating night.

"No, but that was a very unusual event in the first place." She scrubbed a hand over her arm where she'd gotten goose bumps just thinking about the things they'd done while under the psychic influence of his fantasies.

He waved her over to the seat beside him on the chest at the end of the bed. Flickering flames cast shadows over his face, making the angles and hollows more pronounced.

The warm glow burnished his skin with a bronze hue, his hand reaching out to her when she hesitated.

She stared down at it, unsure of her next move. He'd all but come out and said he thought her work was a crock when he'd admitted his main reason for employing her was her PR value.

How could she get any deeper involved with a man who thought so little of her profession?

"Lara." He put his hand down when she didn't come to him. "It seems like we're not going to be able to help each other the way either of us hoped. You won't do the newspaper interview that I wanted, and now you can't provide any other psychic insights into my problems the way you wanted."

"I didn't cash the retainer check." She peered around the room for her purse, prepared to give it all back so they could move on with no regrets or ill will.

"Don't be ridiculous." His arm snaked around her waist now, not waiting for her to come to him on her own. "That fee hardly covers your time away from your own business this weekend, plus you flew up here at a moment's notice."

The feel of his touch damn near made her dizzy. She'd never recover her psychic sensitivities this way. And why did she keep seeing that freaking bread truck?

"But—"

"Keep it. Let's say at this point we don't owe each other one damn thing. We still have the rest of the weekend to fill, no electricity to distract ourselves, and no way of leaving early until the storm dies down. Don't you think we're entitled to at least enjoy—" he ran his hand down her waist to her hip and squeezed "—this?"

A deluge of sensual feelings rained down over the confusion and fears. It would be so easy to get lost in this. In him.

But indulging that temptation wouldn't suddenly make Dex understand her or give him any shred of respect for the kind of work she did. With an effort, she stepped back out of the range of his hands.

"I can't." She would spend the rest of her time reading the family history or searching the halls for any scrap of psychic energy that might be useful even if she couldn't sense things that directly related to Dex.

"So you'll admit on one hand that you feel close to me, but on the other, you won't let yourself explore it or enjoy it?" His handsome face appeared as confused as she felt inside.

But she wouldn't be ruled by sensations that had led her so incredibly far astray before. Even with that huge four-poster bed tempting her to tangle with him in the Egyptian cotton.

"I can't." Her eyes burned and she blinked hard to hold back the emotions threatening to spill over.

Fortunately, the darkness helped her keep her turmoil private because Dex rose to his feet and walked out of her room without a second glance.

10

WORKING ON A LIST of enemies seemed like a shit alternative to having Lara in his bed.

Dex pounded away on the keyboard of his laptop with the two hours' worth of battery he'd had charged before the power went out. At least his Internet connection had come back and he could send some words of encouragement to Massimo who'd loaded his in-box with five messages over the course of ten hours.

Now, as Dex focused his eyes on his list of enemies at 11:02 p.m., his brain wandered far away to Lara's room. Was she in bed yet? He'd checked on her at about seven o'clock to give her a sandwich and a bottle of wine, but she hadn't been in the guest room. He'd left the food on the nightstand and hoped she'd find it, unwilling to hunt for her through the huge house only to get shot down again.

The woman wasn't doing his ego a damn bit of good.

Although…

His hands stilled over the keys where he was in the middle of typing the twenty-third name on his ever-growing list of suspects. She had admitted, in a roundabout way, that she cared for him. According to Lara, her ability to use her psychic senses diminished when she got personally involved with someone.

In this case, him.

Hands falling away from the keyboard, he let that idea wash over him. How many people had ever owned up to caring about him during such a low point in his life? In his experience, women came during the good times when money and influence had rolled his way faster than he could count it all. Women had always been part of the success, the lush rewards for a job well done.

But they'd been as quick to disappear when times were tough. He'd had a girlfriend who dumped him in college because he managed a pizza shop and then made booty calls when he'd started repping their university's quarterback the moment the guy turned eligible. And one of Dex's few steady girlfriends of the last decade—Chrissy—had vanished after his soccer star client made the ill-advised porno tape and articles started appearing questioning Dex's magic touch in the industry.

That had hurt.

Her defection had felt like kicking a guy when he was down, and he'd realized that he'd never gained any real judgment where women were concerned. Twelve years after college, Dex didn't have any better eye for what women really wanted than he'd had as a freshman undergrad. What did that say about him? He could head a huge, successful firm—and despite the recent bout of bad luck, no one would call his business anything but a success overall—but he couldn't see past the end of his nose when it came to females.

Maybe that's why there were a few women's names on

his list of people who might want to do him harm. Chrissy had seemed pissed after they broke up, even though it had been her who dumped him. He remembered now it was because she'd wanted him to fight for her. But at the time, he couldn't understand who in the hell he was supposed to be fighting. Her? It had been her who suggested the split, after all.

Closing the laptop full of too many names representing too many failures, Dex knew now that Chrissy had expected him to wade into deeper relationship waters. She'd wanted him to make a case for their relationship, or at least talk through their problems instead of letting her walk away.

The understanding came too late to salvage things between them, which was just as well since meeting Lara had showed him a whole other dimension to relationships that he hadn't seen before. His connection with Chrissy had been happy. Comfortable. But his bond with vibrant Lara made all other women pale by comparison.

Still, he couldn't help wonder if he could make use of what he'd learned with Chrissy. Women expected effort. A commitment that went beyond mere faithfulness.

Dex didn't understand exactly what he shared with Lara, but there had to be something between them for a woman like her to care about him. Her feelings might be bad news for her, but for Dex, it was the first sign that maybe his luck was beginning to change.

LARA HELD the family genealogy book high above the chlorinated water, balancing the pages on her knees as she perched beside the heated indoor pool she'd discovered on the main level.

She'd found the spot while hunting for as much natural light as possible in the dark mansion. She'd wandered room to room with her book and her candle, looking for as many windows as possible on a side of the house that would benefit from the patchy bits of moonlight occasionally breaking through the cloud cover. She'd found it in this minispa that looked sort of like a Roman bath. The pool was built of dark slate, with columns rising up out of the water. The oval room sported floor-to-ceiling windows on one end that took advantage of the scant moonbeams' reflection on the snow. The light made it less of a strain to read the genealogy book, and she'd been enticed to dip her feet into the heated water that hadn't cooled much since the power went out. She'd worn a pair of pajamas down here, but she'd ditched the bottoms to sit poolside, easily folding the extra fabric of the top under her butt to keep her off the stones.

And as lovely as the water felt around her feet, Lara found it difficult to enjoy with the weight of the Brantley family history on her mind. The curse wasn't referenced in the book that seemed to have been commissioned by the family, but the bad luck certainly had been. Dex's great-grandfather had lost his wife to tuberculosis shortly after his mistress had died, leaving the two children motherless in a home their father never again visited.

The family fortunes suffered, but only until the boys entered the stock market, where they each added substantially to the Brantley clan's coffers. Their riches had been substantial enough, thankfully, to withstand the stock market crash, but only because they'd invested in land. Their finances never fully recovered until their children became successful in other fields, and the pattern of good luck followed by bad continued right up until Dexter had been hit hard on his thirty-third birthday.

"Are you responsible for this?" Lara asked out loud, wondering if the spirit of the dead mistress lurked nearby while her sensitivities were too low to perceive her.

Or while she was too much affected by Dex.

"There you are." Dexter's voice startled her since she hadn't been aware of his footsteps.

But suddenly he was there, a tall and imposing shadow figure on the other side of the room. His broad shoulders nearly filled the door frame, his presence sending an electric current through the quiet room.

She became aware of her bare legs and wished she hadn't slid her pants off to dip her toes. She needed more layers to steel herself against Dex, not less.

"I was looking for some natural light and this room seemed to have the most." Gesturing toward the book, she closed the heavy volume and set it aside. "I've been doing some reading."

He came into better view as he neared her, his face reaching the minimal light that bathed one end of the pool.

"I left you some dinner a couple of hours ago."

"I found it when I went upstairs to change." She smoothed the hem of her navy-blue pajama top down to midthigh. "Thank you."

Waving away her thanks, he sat down beside her and kicked off his leather loafers and socks, then rolled up his pant legs.

"Sorry you have to subsist on deli food all weekend. The chow here is usually a lot better." He plunked his feet down into the water to rest on the long, low step that took up one whole side of the pool.

Their skin took on a ghostly hue under the surface, their feet appearing even closer together than they really were by some trick of the water.

"It's an incredible house, Dex. That book I'm reading on your family talks about how much time and planning went into building it." Looking up into his face, she realized he was closer in real life, too.

Her skin tingled in response, her physical senses all the more keen with her psychic ones quiet.

"Yeah? The taxes are insane. And just keeping the place from crumbling took a boatload of my parents' money. When I made my first million, they were thrilled to hand it over to me and move to a no-maintenance condo in Florida. Some of these old houses were torn down just so the families didn't have to pony up those monster amounts of cash for drafty properties without all the modern extras."

"What a shame." She couldn't imagine dismantling this place with all the history in its walls. Just from sitting on the ledge of the pool, she knew the rock had been brought in by boat from quarries all over Canada. Information she'd perceived *before* he set his sexy self down beside her and rendered her deaf to anything but keen want. "You won't have to do that with this place, will you?"

His financial position had to have suffered when so many of his top athletes had left him or left sports altogether.

"I hope not. It would make it easier if I'd cave to the pressure to show the place a few times a month the way that historical society would like. You get a tax break then, according to this guy who's been pushing the idea."

Lara weighed his words, suspecting Dex was connected to this place in far more ways than its potential as a tax break and for the first time she understood how much he valued his privacy despite his almost obsessive need to stay in touch with his business. Perhaps he valued it all the more *because* his business required so much of him.

"You said he's one of the enemies you've made?" Lara thought an enemy nearby would be the most likely to be responsible for a local crime.

Dex nodded, staring down into the water.

"Apparently he's got a tour boat route that goes right by here and he figures he'd be able to double the ticket price if he could include Brantley House as a stopping point since this is one of the better-kept properties still in use."

She tried to envision this tour boat operator and came up blank. Instead, her mind inserted a man in a bread truck and she wondered if there was more to that vision than she'd initially realized.

Dex flexed his foot in the pool and the resulting swirl of water from his movement brushed around her calves like a phantom touch. That small caress imparted a thrill that sparked all the way up her bare legs.

"How is the list of enemies coming?" She hoped talking business would keep her mind off Dex's hot, all-male presence beside her. "Are there any people who…deliver bread? I keep having this vision of a bread truck and—"

The expression on his face stopped her cold. His jaw fell open and then snapped shut.

"A bread truck caused a pileup on the George Washington Bridge when I had a fender bender last week. Do you think that's what you're seeing? Christ, do you think the driver caused the accident purposely to…cause me intentional injury?"

He appeared surprised, as if he hadn't really considered the idea of the trouble in his life being coldly and calculatingly constructed by someone out to physically harm him.

And even as Lara felt reassured that she hadn't completely lost her psychic senses, she hated the idea of anyone trying to hurt Dex.

"I don't know. I don't see the vehicle in an accident, I just see the driver wearing a uniform with the bread company logo on the breast pocket." A logo she couldn't make out clearly. A face she couldn't discern behind sunglasses.

"I don't remember the bakery. Newman's maybe? Sort of red and yellow?"

"That's it." She couldn't staunch the thrill of getting something right, the pleasure at finding a concrete lead. "You can call the company and find out who would have been driving that day."

"Not that I have any bread truck drivers on my list of enemies, but yeah, I'll definitely check that out."

"How is your list coming?"

"Long. I shut down the computer at twenty-three names. I didn't know how far back to go, timewise. I mean, I figured the kid who I stole my college girlfriend from wouldn't be holding a grudge thirteen years later so I kicked off the list chronologically with my former client Victor Marek. I hoped looking back five years was more than enough."

There was something intimate about talking to him in the dim light over the pool of water that intensified every sound, every movement. The simple rumble of his voice sent a shiver up her spine and she hugged her arms tighter around her waist, clutching the silk nightshirt.

A sense of goodwill and pleasure snaked over her now that she'd at least provided him with some snippet of information that might help him figure out who wanted to sabotage him. Maybe she wouldn't fight this attraction so hard if she could find a way to recover her skills and be with Dex at the same time.

"I forgot you said you two parted ways." She didn't want to think about Dex's clients, but she owed him better than to dump her runaway feelings on him again.

"Vic made a brief recovery in his performance after you worked with him, but then he fell apart again the next season." Dex shrugged, his strong shoulders showing little empathy for someone who didn't work hard.

"And he was mad at you because you wouldn't stick with him through his slump?"

"It wasn't just a slump. I don't mind repping an MLB player with a low batting average or a guy who's always on the disabled list. What gets me are the athletes who get in those mental funks where they're mad at the world, or they're convinced their contract is screwing them. I can't deal with the sense of entitlement that comes from some of the guys. I mean, I'm all for raking in the major bucks, but sometimes they lose sight of just how freaking cool it is to be in the big game and they piss away their time in the limelight being bitter they got a hundred grand less than the latest hotshot rookie."

"Around my office we call it CBS. Crybaby Syndrome. It's an office rule that you have to leave for the day if you've got it, because it's totally contagious."

They shared a grin and the sense of intimacy grew, blooming dark and sweet like a night-blossoming flower. The urge to move toward him, to tangle her wet legs against his, was almost unbearable.

"So how large is your office? I thought your Web site said something about changing locations."

She blinked at the question, surprised she could be floundering in the throes of lust while he asked innocuous questions about her work. Still, she had pushed him away the last time, concerned for her dwindling psychic powers and—more than likely—a little afraid of where this attraction might lead.

At least one of those concerns had diminished a bit in light of her vision of the bread truck driver. Might she be learning to control her emotions enough to retain some of her extrasensory abilities with Dex?

"I just moved from working out of my home to a real office in a converted carriage house outside Albany. The space is beautiful and we have our own gardens overlooking a small, man-made lake, but it's just my assistant and me." Lara wondered what Jamie would think of Dex if the two of them met in person. Tough to guess how a ghost-hunting computer geek would view an iron-pumping business dynamo.

"Just the two of you?" Dex shifted in the water, turning toward her on the stone edge of the pool so that his knee grazed her hip. "I seem to remember your assistant is male. Nothing romantic there, I hope?"

"No." She'd met Jamie at a psi conference when he'd been telling fortunes with a crystal ball as a laugh. "That's an unspoken office rule since I think romance leads to problems when people are working—together."

Her cheeks warmed at the admission.

"Are you speaking from experience?" His eyes took on a shimmering heat.

"I didn't mean us, necessarily," she said quickly. "I had a bad experience getting involved with a clairvoyant I worked for when I was finishing up my psych degree."

Sebastian had been a highly regarded guest speaker on parapsychology and she'd been attracted to him immediately. His offer of an internship after she graduated had seemed like a golden opportunity.

"Please don't say I look just like him or otherwise remind you of this guy."

"No." The two men had nothing in common other than their unique ability to rob her of her extra senses. "He was deeply enmeshed in the psi world and—I understand now—fancied himself sort of a kingpin in our community. But he was the only other man who ever created the same kind of psychic blind spot for me that you do."

"What happened?" He casually swirled his hand through the water in a lazy circle even though she suspected he listened carefully to her response.

"Apparently, while my psychic senses went down the toilet around him, his only increased with our growing connection. So he could read me like a book while I was left more blind than usual." The situation had sucked her in for a while, when he'd used his enhanced abilities to be exactly the kind of lover she wanted in a man, even charming her conservative mother. "Eventually, he would read my thoughts and impressions as I prescreened his clients and use my observations as the readings he gave to those same clients, basically making me do his work for him and expending no effort of his own to maintain his business while he wrote books and gave workshops for hefty speaker fees."

He shook his head, not bothering to hide his disgust. "You did his work for no credit."

"Yes. And worse, I didn't even realize it because I couldn't read him. It took me months to figure out why I was mentally and emotionally drained all the time." She'd been a total wreck, strung out, exhausted and—finally— brokenhearted that she'd lost a man who'd meant so much to her. She'd been too naive to see that she'd meant little to him in return.

And—surprise, surprise—her mother had been furious with her for letting such a great catch slip away.

Dex's hand landed on her knee, warm and wet with pool water. The shock of his touch cut straight through the old hurts, soothing them away.

"I'm sorry you went through that." His thumb stroked a hot path around her kneecap before dipping behind her leg to the hollow there. "But you have to know that when you're blinded like that—when you can't use your extra senses—that's the way the rest of us go through relation- ships all the time. We're blind that way with every single person that comes along, clueless about the other person's intentions and doing our best to muddle through."

His words comforted her, or maybe it was just the se- ductive feel of his hand on her as he scooped another handful of heated pool water and poured it over her legs. Droplets trickled down her calves while a few rolled back down her thighs.

She imagined his touch everywhere the water went, her gaze fixed on his strong, glistening hand.

"I find it hard to believe that you've ever had to stumble your way through a relationship."

His fingers began to track the path of the warm water, gliding up the inside of her thigh. Her breath stuck in her throat and she sat utterly still, watching.

"That's because it's my job to look like a guy on top of my game." Steam rolled up off the water, or maybe it was rising off of her.

She certainly felt hot enough.

"So you're admitting that you are a professional BS artist?" Her breasts tightened, her chest rising and falling faster in anticipation of his touch even though she'd tried damn hard to suppress her feelings.

"That's not quite the spin I'd put on it, but let me assure you, I feel like I'm running blind with you, too, because I don't have a clue where I stand."

The sincerity in his voice spoke to something deep inside her, some feminine instinct that had more to do with her heart than her third eye. She wanted to believe him, needed to believe him, even as she recognized that need had shoved her over the edge and into an abyss of sweet emotions.

"It scares me." Her admission didn't stop her from laying her hand over his where he touched her, her gaze locked on his bronzed fingers stretched over her pale thigh.

"I'm right there with you," he muttered, his breath so close to her ear the words warmed her skin.

And she knew at that moment—her psychic senses be damned—she had to be with him this one last time. She would leave Brantley Island tomorrow, when the storm cleared and the police arrived.

She wouldn't take his money, wouldn't let him turn her stay into his personal PR campaign. But she had to experience this amazing chemistry with Dexter once more. Because no matter how much emotional insight she picked up from reading a person's thoughts or understanding their past, no psychic connection could compare to the increased physical sensitivity Dex made her feel with one electrifying touch.

11

HE FLEXED HIS FINGERS against her smooth skin, restraining himself in all ways but that one. He wanted her to come to him, wanted her to make the decision to be with him.

But that meant stuffing down a hundred other urges, all of which had to do with pulling his sexy psychic down into the water with him and peeling off her damp nightshirt. Ever since he'd walked into the spa area, he'd been fantasizing about letting the gentle whirling current of the lap pool wash over her naked body. He wanted to see her come undone in the moonlight, wanted to spread her legs wide while he tasted her wetness, wanted to feel her all around him while she cried out his name again and again.

None of that was going to happen if Lara didn't make the next move. He considered himself damn near a saint for keeping his thoughts to himself aside from that brief stretch of his fingers against her damp skin.

She pulled her gaze up to his and he waited, watching her. Steam curled up from the warm water, drifting along her body clad in a navy-blue silk pajama top that was already sliding off her shoulder.

The moment weighed heavily on him as he waited for her to make the next move. On the other side of the room, the door slammed shut as if locking them in. In quick succession, Dex heard doors slam all over the sprawling house as if a fierce wind had whipped through the whole dwelling.

He tensed, alert for any possible danger. But Lara never even broke eye contact.

"I think it's the ghos—energy forces in the house," she whispered. "Would you think I'm crazy if I said I believe they want us to be together?"

"I don't care what the damn ghosts want." The fire that he'd been stuffing down inside him threatened to consume him whole. "I only care what you want tonight."

Lights burned behind his eyes and he thought he couldn't hold back another second. Soon he wouldn't be able to walk away.

"You." Lara lifted her hand to smooth damp fingers down his cheek. "I just want you to make the heat burn everything else off."

He wasn't sure if he let her get all the words out or if he'd kissed the last few into silence. His mouth landed on hers with none of the teasing skill he showed to other women. This kiss was hot and out of control, his tongue stroking hers with unrestrained hunger.

Impatiently, he worked the buttons on her top, snapping one off in his hurry. She shoved his shirt off his shoulders and moved to his belt, letting him wrestle the shirtsleeves off his wrists. When the gentle brush of her fingers against his fly threatened his sanity, he broke off the kiss and stood to remove his pants. Boxers.

Lara stared up at him, her own body naked now except for black panties that shielded her sex. Her breasts swayed free, her curves supple and pale in the watery reflection from the pool.

His head was on fire with her and all the ways he wanted her. She reached for him, tracing a path down the front of his shaft with two silky fingers, but he couldn't allow himself to be distracted now.

She wanted to feel everything else burn away, and he intended to give her that. Slipping into the water, he tugged her down onto the wide pool steps so the surface reached her breasts.

Bending over her he lashed at one rosy peak with his tongue, unable to get enough of her. Her back arched immediately to press herself closer, unabashedly asking for more. He slid one arm around her waist, drawing her hips tight against his and grinding.

Her moans echoed in the high chamber, bouncing off the stone columns until her desire was amplified all around him. He rolled her nipple between his teeth and she squeezed her thighs around one of his, riding up his leg in silent demand.

Feeling her heart race there, hot and insistent between her legs, Dex pushed against her, bending his knee and lifting her partially out the water again. She glistened like a mermaid come to life, her wet hair plastered to her shoulders and breasts. Seating her on a higher step, he hooked a finger in her panties and drew them down her legs until they floated away.

Her breath snagged in her throat, her fingers trolling restlessly over his chest and abs. The heat and the water intensified the scent of her, the spicy florals that were strong and exotic like her. The fragrance drugged him as he sank lower into the water to kiss her breasts and belly. He lingered over the depression in her navel, swirling his tongue in circles there, fascinated with the way the water pooled.

Her hips lifted, back arched as a little cry escaped her. And with such a sweet invitation, he couldn't delay any longer. His mouth fell on her sex, tongue delving between the folds for the full taste of her. A soft squeal accompanied a sudden, reflexive spasm in her legs, the muscles tightening on either side of his shoulders.

He gripped her feet under the water and her toes curled against his hands. She was so sweetly responsive, so hot against his tongue. He stroked her with increasing pressure, eager to feel her reach her peak but wanting to draw out the pleasure so that when she came, the whole world rocked around her.

Her breath bordered on hyperventilation. Her legs shifted, thighs pressing against him. She flexed her fingers in his hair, nails digging ever so slightly in a hint of desperation that pleased him to no end. He spread her legs wider, holding her where he wanted her while he worked her, faster, harder, deeper.

She found her release in the white-hot center of it all, her body convulsing with the force of it as he slowed his pace without ceasing. He savored every sweet tremor, every delicate shudder that continued to rock her body afterward.

Only when she quieted completely did he release her. Their eyes met in the moonlit haze and he wondered if it was just the mind-numbing attraction they shared that made him feel so incredibly connected to this woman.

Or was it something much, much deeper?

LARA HAD NEVER CONSIDERED herself a highly sexed woman. She'd had a few lovers, but when those relationships ended, she'd missed the warm camaraderie of having a man in her life far more than the sex.

But dear God, sex with Dex wasn't like that. A woman could become addicted in no time. She suddenly understood the nature of the booty calls that her girlfriends swore were sometimes necessary just for some hormonal adjustment. She wished Dex would be available for the rest of her life to do nothing but this to her.

The satisfaction he'd given her was so sharp and intense that she thought she should need days to recover, but in reality, she already wanted to feel him deep inside her.

"Dex." She looked up at him with her half-formed wishes dancing around her head, wondering if he'd read her wants all over again.

Then again, she wouldn't mind taking charge if she needed to. A vision of herself sitting high atop the massive erection he sported sent pleasurable tingles clear to her toes.

"Yes?" His hand brushed her belly before skating around to her back. His fingers worked their way up her spine and then back down, cupping her bottom.

"I want to feel you inside me."

Her words felt as naked and vulnerable as the rest of her, her breath hitching as she spoke.

"Soon." He'd left a condom at the pool's edge when he'd taken off his pants, but he didn't reach for it yet.

Instead, he lifted her, spinning her around so that her back pressed to his chest as they stood. The feel of steely muscle sent shivers through her as he guided her toward the pool wall, the water only hip-deep near the stairs. She had no idea what he had in mind until he positioned her near one of the jets, adjusting the nozzle so water pulsed hard between her thighs.

She tensed, the pressure an unexpected surprise. But he pushed her forward, his hips guiding hers where he wanted her to be, forcing her squarely in front of that powerful stream.

He cupped her breasts in his hands, bending her forward so the soft mounds filled his palms. The sensations built too fast for her to appreciate every nuance, the pressure between her thighs already growing to a sweetly unbearable level. Dex kicked her feet wider apart, forcing her lower into the water and changing the way the jet stream raced past her swollen sex.

All at once, she flew apart, her whole body spasming with the force of one shuddering orgasm after another. Her knees collapsed, but he held her up, keeping her body perfectly aligned with the maddeningly impersonal lick of water that brought her one climax after another.

Her body was so hungry for him by now she thought she would weep with it, but he lifted her out of the water. Scooping up the condom, he carried her to a wide chaise lounge, his body cast in stark shadow now that they'd moved away from the moonlit windows by the pool.

His tall, angular silhouette made her breath catch, his frame so strong and dominant. The sight of him looming over her reminded her she was physically safe, but dear God she'd never been more emotionally helpless.

She watched him roll on a condom and her insides ached for him. The orgasms that he'd given her had only made her more hungry for this, her feminine muscles squeezing repeatedly around emptiness when she had wanted to be filled. Stretched. Completed.

A chill swept over her for a moment, the water on her skin cooling. And then he was there, on top of her, kissing her, heating her body outside and in. She rolled her hips against him, so ready for him she couldn't wait another instant. In answer, he lifted her thigh high alongside his hip, opening her.

She felt the thick heat of him pressing, nudging, rubbing against her. Her eyes fell shut, all of her senses concentrated on this new level of awareness he'd taken her to before he'd even come inside her. She reached for him, pleading with small sighs she couldn't contain, entreating his cock with a slow stroke of her hand.

Finally, he slid inside, working his hips against her as he pressed harder and then harder still. She gasped from the shock of pleasure, the sensations so sweetly keen she thought she'd die of it.

But then he withdrew from her and the friction made her ache despite her slick heat. As he reentered her, the pleasure built all over again, higher than the last time.

Lara held on to him, her hands searching for a hold on his strong back, her fingers gripping his shoulders as he thrust into her again and again.

She looked up into his eyes, seeing only a glimmer of them in the dark. Technically, she couldn't see into them, but she felt his gaze as surely as any touch and that connection lit her up inside.

"I can't stop thinking about you," he whispered, his breathing ragged with the effort of holding back. "You're the best thing that's happened to me since my luck went bad, Lara."

She tilted her hips up, taking more of him. All of him.

"Maybe the curse is breaking." She kissed his lips, running her tongue over his mouth. "Because you don't feel like a cursed man to me."

"No?" He changed the angle that he entered her, guiding her legs to wrap around his waist while he picked up speed.

"No. You feel amazing. More like a—" her body tightened all around him "—godsend."

She just barely eked the words out before sensations swept through her, racking her body with sweet, shuddering spasms of pleasure. She cried out but Dex caught the sound with his kiss, covering her mouth with his.

Legs locked tight around his hips, she held him deep inside her, knowing that it might be the last time. And heaven help her, she planned to store up every passionate memory from her weekend as Dexter Brantley's lover to keep her warm in the cold days ahead.

IT SAID A LOT ABOUT LARA that Dex could have easily fallen asleep with a smile on his face despite rumors of a curse hanging over his head, an arsonist following him around, a hole in his roof, his company losing money and the most uncomfortable furniture in the world digging into his hip.

In spite of all that, he couldn't help this absurd sense that all was right with the world just because Lara Wyland lay in his arms, warm and soft and sweetly scented. Her breath eased into an even rhythm, her eyes closed. Looking down at her, he felt damn privileged to hold her. She was special.

Unique.

And not the kind of woman he ever would have imagined himself drooling over. His other lovers had been more outwardly sophisticated women with careers in fields that overlapped his. He dated polished women who worked in press offices or sports management. But Lara's style ran between earthy and eclectic, and her work wasn't anything that had ever interested him until she made him think about it—forced him to reevaluate his preconceived notions.

And now here he was, in danger of salivating on her temple as he watched her in the flickering light of the candle he'd retrieved a few minutes ago.

"So what made you become a psychic?" He stroked her hair away from her face as her eyes flickered open again, focusing on him. "Is that something you're just born with, or do you also have to train yourself somehow?"

He was consumed with curiosity about her suddenly, hungry to understand every last detail. No matter what happened after this weekend with his life—whether his cursed status changed or not—he wanted to see Lara again.

"You can do either—train for it or just work with a natural gift. Ideally, psychics have both since even the strongest skills benefit from training and practice." She seemed comfortable giving that portion of the answer, but she paused after that, biting her lip as if she wasn't sure how much to share with him. "I didn't discover my gift until I was a teenager."

"Did you freak out your friends by telling their futures?"

He tried to imagine what it would be like to read people's minds and wondered if she'd applied her skills in Vegas yet.

"I freaked them out all right." Her whole demeanor changed, as if someone had switched off the fuel that lit her from within.

"What happened?" He tensed, wishing he could have kept hurt away from her.

"My best friend's father went missing and I kept seeing him in my dreams." She looked out into the darkness of the room, her eyes focused on a time that wasn't here. "At first I thought I was just worried about him and that's why I kept seeing Mr. Caldwell when I closed my eyes. But then I started dreaming of him—dead."

Dex stifled a wince, hurting for the way she'd suffered back then.

"Hell."

"I knew what happened." Lara turned toward him, her eyes earnest as if willing him to believe her. "It took me a few nights to piece together the dreams, but finally I understood that he'd gotten into a fight with an unstable contractor who'd been building their new house and the guy had killed him during a dispute about Mr. Caldwell's wife."

"Did you go to the police?" He tried to think what he would have done as a teenager.

He kissed her temple, letting his lips linger there.

"No. I went to my mother because she was gifted in that way and I thought she'd know what to do." Lara shivered and he tightened his hold on her. "She took me out into the woods where I knew the body was buried and told me I should find it before we called the police."

His stomach went cold, his fingers ceasing their rhythmic stroking of her hair.

"Please tell me you refused to do that."

Lara shrugged. "Mom said cops never believe our kind of truth, so we had to give them a truth they could understand."

"So you dug up a dead body?" He wondered if he'd be able to yank his jaw back off the sofa.

What the hell kind of mother put her kid through something like that?

"I was worried about destroying evidence, and then, as my mom started digging, I worried even more about what she would say if I was wrong. My whole life, she'd encouraged me to search for my gifts, but I'd always avoided thinking about that stuff because Mom was so passionate about it. Our house was full of herbs and crystals, anything to enhance her power. She wore turbans to all my soccer games." Lara glanced up at him as if accustomed to comments on her mother's choice of headgear.

But Dex was still stuck on the dead body.

"Did you find it?"

"Mom did." Her voice dipped lower, her eyes softening their focus as if she had looked back to the past again. "We recognized Mr. Caldwell's wedding ring on the left hand."

"Jesus." He couldn't begin to picture how that must have felt.

Lara spun in his arms to face him, her hair spilling off her shoulder onto the chaise behind her.

"She told me that while I had done well to finally acknowledge my gift, I would have done better to heed it sooner in the process so that I could find missing people alive instead of—" she gestured with her hand, making a vague spinning motion as if she could churn the word out by force "—dead."

Her voice broke and Dex couldn't even believe the guilt trip that had been unloaded on Lara's young shoulders. A guilt trip that obviously found its target since she maintained a business that did exactly as her mother had bidden.

"Honey, I'm so sorry." He wrapped her tight in his arms and kissed the top of her head, wishing she'd never felt that kind of hurt. "You know that wasn't your fault any more than it's a police officer's fault when someone dies. Hell, it's less your fault since you weren't even on the job."

"Maybe not, but I have come to respect my mother's point." She freed herself from his hold enough to look up at him, her eyes clear and resolute. Calmer now. "I can't sit back and do nothing when people go missing and I'm able to help. It's important work, even if the victim's family doesn't recognize it or believe in it."

He wondered how many other gruesome scenes she'd witnessed in her visions, how many other people she'd been terrified for because of her abilities.

"I saw that on your Web site when I looked you up again." He seemed to be discovering a whole different side of her, a side that he'd been completely blind to the first time they'd met. "I was surprised because I just assumed you did more work like the kind Victor hired you for—small-time stuff like doing readings for people or helping them with personal problems."

He'd kind of envisioned her on the other end of a 1-800-PSYCHIC number, surprising people with insights that were keen but not necessarily psychic.

"No. The smaller work finances the bigger jobs that are important to me. If we could have come to agreeable terms this weekend, my fee could have given me another month to work on missing persons cases."

Whether she meant it as a jab or not, he certainly felt the sting. He shifted their positions, and the feel of her damp skin against his fired a renewed hunger for her, even as their conversation treaded into more risky terrain.

"So why can't we come to terms?" He figured it couldn't hurt to make one last pitch, especially now that they'd experienced such closeness. "Why can't you let the newspaper article serve as publicity for your business so that more people can find you?"

"Because I'm already taking flak from family and friends for using my skills in a way they view as no better than a carnival sideshow. Every time I take on a case helping someone with their personal life or assisting someone with a past life regression just for fun, they see it as me frittering away my talents."

"But you're not."

"I agree. But it does suck to be perceived that way." She paused, gnawing her lip for a moment before plowing ahead. "So you can see where it would suck even more to be hired for completely frivolous reasons like serving as someone's PR momentum when the client doesn't even put any faith in my skills."

The temperature in the room dropped so fast Dex wondered how he could be freezing his butt off when he'd been burning inside a short while ago. She'd nailed him with an accusation that had been totally accurate two short days ago. No matter that he'd come to understand her work with different eyes now. He still couldn't deny the large amount of truth in her concern even though he was trying to see her differently.

Damn it, he did see her differently.

But if he couldn't prove it to her, if he couldn't show some belief in her methods and support for the things that were important to her, she would be kicking him to the curb faster than he could say "cynic."

12

LARA WASN'T TRYING to give Dex a hard time.

Although, as she observed the swift changes in his expression, she supposed she could see where it might seem like that. But damn it, she couldn't just ignore an opportunity to make him understand why she didn't want him touting her presence in his life in every major media outlet.

Her work didn't need the three-ring circus the extra attention would bring.

"Do you really think you're here for frivolous reasons, Lara?" Dex shifted beside her as he waved his hand around, gesturing to the room. "Every door in this house closed at the same time earlier. You saw the ghost of my great-grandfather's lover in the stairwell. You uncovered a possible murder. Does that sound frivolous to you?"

His tone was hard, bordering on mad. But without her extra sensitivities where he was concerned, that was all she could interpret about his mood. Was it easy for him to morph from bone-melting closeness to this icy distance? She honestly didn't know.

Levering up on her arm, she sat on the chaise and tugged a towel from a stack nearby. An hour ago, she'd been itching to come out of her clothes, but right now she welcomed the terry cloth coverage. Their conversation had left her too exposed.

"It doesn't matter what I think." Her heart stung, knowing he didn't really understand what she wanted. Needed. "Just because I believe I spoke with a spirit doesn't mean *you* believe it, and it doesn't mean you feel any differently about my role here. You still see my presence as some kind of defensive business move. And while I applaud your ability to think outside the box with creative problem solving, I can't fix problems you don't accept as existing. I can't perform parlor tricks for the media to make them think everything is okay with you when it isn't."

She rose from the chaise, needing the protection of clothes, needing space. Dexter's silence followed her to beside the pool where she shrugged her way into her pajama top, the quiet telling her that no matter how many barriers she put between them, the damage to her heart had already been done.

Outside the spa area, a telephone rang in the hallway. The old-fashioned ring suggested it was a corded phone and not an electric model, the power still out all through the house.

Lara stood out of the way as Dex marched by her to answer it, her fingers feeling around the far end of the pool until she fished her panties out the water, wrung them out and stuffed them in her pocket.

"Damn it." Dex growled at the door and he tugged on it, jiggling the knob.

"Is it stuck?" Foreboding tingled over her even without her extra senses where Dex was concerned.

"No. It feels more like it's locked." He slammed his shoulder into the barrier while the phone rang again and again. "Do ghosts lock doors? Is that something else on my list of things to believe?"

Lara didn't answer. She knew throwing hurtful words around wouldn't take away the real pain they were both feeling. Instead, she turned to look out the window into the night. She could almost feel the chill rolling off the thin layer of icy snow covering the ground.

Shivering, she reached for her pajama pants and slid them on, but that didn't take away the cold. The ringing phone finally ceased, but Dex's pounding didn't. Strangely, the sound of his beating on the door seemed to recede, growing softer as the room chilled even more.

And then Lara knew a presence had entered the room.

She tried to methodically observe the physical reactions of her body, the instincts that let her know a spirit had joined them, but it had happened too fast for her to read those signs.

"Lara."

The feminine voice called to her from the bank of windows where snow suddenly swirled up from the ground outside.

Distantly, Lara could still hear Dex growling at the door and heaving his weight against the hundred-year-old barrier. But her focus remained on the other energy that hovered just outside the spa room.

"Did you do this?" Lara whispered to the spirit, hoping Dex wouldn't overhear and have more reason to believe she was a kook. "Did you lock us in here?"

"I locked *him* in." She sounded put out, her voice bordering on a whine despite the aristocratic diction. "He is so locked in his own perspectives, I thought it only fitting to lock him in physically."

"That really isn't—"

"You'll find *you're* not locked in, my dear." The voice sounded as if it were smiling, although the figure never took a real shape outside in the snow. "You can lead him through until he understands what he must do to set himself free. These arrogant Brantley men have always been too concerned about public perception. That's most of the reason dear Willy never could admit what really happened on the stairs…."

"Lara." Dex's voice was raised, the sharp tone shattering her concentration on the other voice.

She turned away from the window where the snow had grown still once again.

"Yes?"

"I'm going to take the hinges off." He'd put his pants on at some point, although his feet remained bare and his chest uncovered. "Do you have anything in your pockets that might help? Change or keys?"

She walked toward the door, curious to see if the spirit's words were true or if the locked door was truly a problem.

"The only thing in my pockets is my underwear from last night." She approached the door as Dex warned her away from it.

"It's locked, you know." He stepped closer. "If I can't open it—"

Snick.

The handle turned easily for her, the door opening instantly.

"How the hell did you do that?"

She didn't have a clue how to answer that one. The moment reminded her of so many others in her life—times she didn't fit in, times she made other people uncomfortable. Stalling, she picked up the Brantley family history book she'd been reading and figured she find her room to try and get some rest before daybreak.

Heaven knew, she was wasting her time searching for acceptance from a man who didn't understand her any better than the rest of the world at large.

"Honestly, Dex, you wouldn't believe me if I told you."

THERE HAD TO BE ANOTHER explanation for this. The curse, the locked doors, the roof caving in, everything.

Dex stomped through the house for half an hour looking for answers, full of purpose as he checked out the rooms for some sign of tampering with the doors. Some sign of sabotage or breaking and entering would help him end this hellish year of his life once and for all.

He knew there had to be a reasonable explanation as sure as he knew the NFL draft was going to make or break him this year. He couldn't afford to stay in a business with no big clients.

Massimo was his last hope professionally just as Lara had been his last hope personally. She was so easy to be around. So accepting of him even when he took phone calls in the middle of a sentence. Damn it, why couldn't he be as accepting of her in return?

He paused in the course of pulling on a pair of boots by the side entrance that led to the boathouse and the tennis courts. He'd been thinking about checking the out-

buildings for signs of a trespasser, some clue that they'd
been locked into the spa area intentionally, but the direction of his thoughts gave him pause.

Lara wasn't really to blame for not following through
on his larger plan. He should have made her aware of it
before he enticed her up here thinking he wanted her to—
do whatever it was she did for other clients who were
cursed. Funny how he'd never really asked her that; he'd
been so focused on his own plan of attack he hadn't
bothered to find out if she might really be able to help him
with her unusual gifts.

Damn it.

He'd messed things up with her and he couldn't see a
way to make it right. He couldn't fake an endorsement of
her methods when he was so tied into finding rational explanations for everything that had happened to him, and
she wouldn't accept his cynicism when it came to her
work. Maybe he should just let her leave instead of tor-
menting them both with the possibility of a future they
wouldn't be able to create.

Jamming a hat on his head and his arms into his coat
sleeves, Dex stepped outside in the still hours before dawn.
He'd check the outbuildings in a minute, but first he'd see
if the conditions had died down enough to take the boat
out for a trip to the mainland.

He swallowed down the burn of regret at the idea of her
leaving. The storm had stopped by nightfall and the St.
Lawrence River appeared unnaturally calm. With the wind
dying down and the sky clearing, the only sign of the
storm was the thin coating of icy snow on the ground.

He really shouldn't have gotten so worked up over Lara

being able to open the door when he couldn't. She'd freaked him out, big-time. But that wasn't her fault.

God, he'd been a jackass in so many ways this weekend. Maybe he'd been a sports agent for too many years if he was trying to bring his wheeling-and-dealing ways into his personal life. For years he'd thought women came and went with the rise and fall of his career, but was that really the case?

Maybe he was simply too driven—too tied to his job when his business struggled. More to the point, maybe he'd just been too much distracted with work during those times to maintain any kind of relationship. He may have pushed women away without even realizing it.

His boots paused in their crunching trek toward the boathouse to process the weight of that realization. At his feet, a small snow squall stirred, lifting the heavy accumulation and swirling it around despite the lack of wind anywhere else on the island. Dex watched it whirl for a moment before it fell back to the ground in fresh, powdery flakes, settling again as if it never moved.

"Weird freaking weather." Shaking his head, he forged ahead across the lawns, passing the stone archways that led to a variety of gardens he hadn't bothered to keep up this last year. The island was really beautiful, deserving of better care than he gave it.

He needed to seriously revisit his priorities before he lost everything that meant something to him.

Opening the door to the boathouse, he figured he would pull his remaining speedboat out into the main water. He wouldn't hold Lara here if she didn't want to help him. Since its twin had been stolen, however, Dex wanted to look it over more carefully now to be sure no damage had been done.

With no moonlight to illuminate the building, Dex had to feel along the wall until his eyes adjusted to the dimness. He snagged his skin on some rough wood, but eventually turned the corner and strode back to the motorboat's docking area.

And there, where his smallest boat should have been, sat an empty slip.

The ropes lay in sloppy piles across the deck, one frayed end dipping in the water. But there was no boat in sight.

"Lara."

His feet were moving before his fears had time to fully form. He needed to find her, needed to warn her something more was at work in the house this weekend than strange energy and old ghosts.

Jesus.

"Lara!" He shouted her name as he ran out of the boat-house and across the grounds toward the mansion.

LARA WAS PULLING ON a long sweater and jeans when a sudden, tangible fear gripped her heart.

She jolted, bumping into a table behind her and knocking over her candles. The room went dark and silent except for her breathing.

"Dex?" What had just happened? She didn't have any visions, no conversations with spirits, no signs of a precognitive episode. Just this sudden palpable fear that something was wrong.

When she'd had the vision of the bread truck driver she'd thought that the larger threat to Dex would be on the mainland, in a big city where she pictured such a truck.

But now she knew the threat was here. Imminent. Fear clogged her throat even though she didn't see anyone, couldn't hear anything out of the ordinary.

Moving toward the window, she pulled the curtains back to let in the light from the oncoming dawn. She scrambled to find her cell phone, reeling from one piece of furniture to the next to find it.

She had to warn Dex. And hell, she had to get out of here. Bolting from the room, a strong man's arms wrapped around as soon as she stepped into the corridor.

She screamed, but her mouth was flattened against a bulging bicep and no noise escaped. The wind went out of her lungs as the man's other arm squeezed her middle, suffocating her with his strength. Instantly she knew the man who held her was the man who'd cut the rope tie, the angry man of her visions.

Too late, she recognized him as the same man who'd hired her five years ago when she'd first met Dex. A man who squeezed her so hard now that her legs went weak and her whole body tingled with the lack of oxygen until she slumped senseless in his arms.

SHE'D BEEN SO EASY to overpower he almost felt cheated.

Victor watched over Lara's still form in the bottom of the boat as he rowed them out to the middle of the river and around a small island west of Brantley's place. At first he thought he'd killed her when he'd dumped her in the boat and she hadn't even winced when he knocked her head against a metal seat. But she was breathing, just unconscious.

Her initial struggles hadn't even made him break a sweat. After years of college football and time in the NFL, he could bench-press three times this woman's weight. Had he made a mistake in taking her instead of Dex? Victor had the size advantage, but he knew Dex was no lightweight. The guy worked out like an athlete, his home fitness center the kind of hard-core facility any gym rat would love.

But he'd have his showdown with Dex eventually. For now he had Dex's lady love to apply the psychological torment, something he knew was more devastating than physical pain.

Now, dipping his oars into the water with mechanical precision, Victor tried to take some satisfaction from what he'd accomplished so far. It was tough, though. He was born to play football, not mind games with a big shot agent who didn't care about his athletes. But Dex Brantley had robbed Vic of his beloved sport, the one reprieve from his crappy family, the one thing in life that ever brought Vic any real joy.

Even his father had paid attention when Vic played. His NFL career had been the sole source of positive communication between him and his old man, and now it was gone. With no Sunday games to sober up for, Vic's father didn't even take a break in the nonstop bingeing that would propel him to an early grave.

Then his shady cousin had shown up with the spy gadgets he used as a P.I. and helped Vic figure out a way to take Dex down. The way his cousin talked, a hit was kid's play if you planned it right. And since when did Vic wuss out of anything? If his cousin Harold could do it, Victor damn well could.

His family had steered him right here, to this moment, to the life of crime he'd tried to avoid.

Screw Brantley and his lightweight chick.

Victor would right the wrong that had been done to him and too many other players who were viewed as money machines for their agents and not human beings. The buck stopped here. Today. The industry had lost its bearings in a bid for fat incomes and steroid-induced perfection on the field. Vic would make Brantley—and by example, his colleagues who were as corrupt as him—see that sports needed a human face again.

And as much as Victor hated to flex his muscle with a woman a quarter of his size, he needed to sacrifice Lara Wyland to drive a message home to the high-and-mighty Brantley. Everyone had their breaking point and it was past time for Dex the Hex to feel what it was like to reach that place of total despair.

13

"I DON'T CARE what the conditions are." Dex tried not to yell at the local park police dispatcher as he juggled a cell phone and attempted to untie another boat that had been dry-docked for the winter. "A woman has been kidnapped, possibly worse. I need search teams out here now."

Hell, he needed a helicopter and the U.S. Coast Guard, but he didn't think he was going to get them by staying on the phone with the park police. Too many agencies had a hand in patrolling the St. Lawrence with its international waters, making it impossible to figure out who had jurisdiction over what.

"Mr. Brantley, I'll send someone out to you as soon as possible, but with the fog, the conditions are extremely dangerous and it takes time to—"

"Fine." He pressed one of the buttons with his cheek as he started the lift to lower the boat into the water. Thank God the power had come back on. He needed every advantage he could get. "Thank you."

For all the fat lot of help she'd been.

Damn the freaking weather. Dex had searched the whole island, every room in the mansion and every out-building from the cabana to the stables, a feat that had taken him almost two hours in the layer of wet snow and ice since he couldn't seem to get any help out here.

He'd found no trace of Lara, but his Athlete's Room had been destroyed. Every jersey, framed poster, award, pennant and trophy had been stripped from the walls and shelves, the whole room a defiled mess.

Whoever had taken Lara had also sabotaged the rest of his life, and the scumbag obviously hated Dex on a deep, personal level to trash everything he'd worked for over the past decade.

Fury boiled inside him as he dialed directory assistance for help reaching the Coast Guard. He'd hire a private chopper if he had to, but somebody was going to start scouring the waters around Brantley Island to find her.

And oh God, the notion stabbed him in the gut, twisting at the soft places inside him. If this person did anything to hurt Lara. Hell, why take Lara in the first place?

To hurt him.

The answer was so obvious he didn't need to be psychic. What he did need was backup, some sense of direction to start his search, and enough clearheaded focus to get the job done effectively. After hardly sleeping for two nights, his brain was sluggish from continuous hours of being awake when he needed to be sharp.

Finally, the craft was in the water and he filled the tank with gas. He'd chosen this boat because it had global positioning satellite technology that would help him navigate around the islands. He didn't want to think about the other reason he might need this particular one he normally used for fishing trips.

With depth sounder technology, the watercraft could

sense below the surface to find fish and show the specks of red moving across the electronic readout. If anything else lurked beneath the surface of the waterway like—God help him—a body, the fish finder would indicate a solid mass in the water.

Dex's vision blurred at the thought, his head filled with worst-case scenarios that would only cloud his judgment. He'd nearly lost his mind when he'd gotten back in the house and she wasn't there. His heart had been running on fast-forward ever since. He couldn't let anything happen to her.

The phone droned in his ear again, the digital voice giving him the number he needed. He punched the numbers into his cell memory with a sense of accomplishment. They would listen to him, damn it. However, he wanted to get the boat in the water first because he suspected the call might go long with bureaucratic runaround. At least he could be searching while he made his case over the phone. The ice storm had cleared enough that someone should be able to get out here.

Once he got the boat out into open water and set up the GPS, he would put in a call to the Coast Guard and one to a friend with a chopper service. Hopefully one of them would provide a solid lead—fast. Because for now, he could only rely on his gut. He sure could use some of Lara's intuitiveness right about now.

He didn't know how or where to find her, but he *would* find her. Now that this prick who had it in for him had taken Lara, the games were over. One way or another, the Brantley curse ended today.

LARA HAD NEVER EXPERIENCED astral dreaming—dreams where your spirit left your body and roamed free to explore the world.

But she sure hoped she was experiencing the phenomenon now, because either that or she was dying. She seemed to float over her body lying in the bottom of a small motorboat that her captor rowed with oars. She could see the man who'd taken her—Victor Marek, the NFL kicker who'd been Dex's client. He'd been the man she'd seen in her visions, but she hadn't processed enough of the images to make the connection.

Although she was curious why he would try to hurt her—hurt Dex—Lara couldn't find it in herself to rouse from whatever deep sleep held her captive in the bottom of the boat. It seemed far easier to fly away from the unpleasantness, to let her spirit soar higher and higher until she could see the islands as dots in the river below her. Brantley Island sat, regal and lonely, to the west. Off to one side of the property, a boat bobbed in the water. A man slumped down in the padded seats, his dark hair vivid against the white leather bolsters lining the boat's benches.

Dex.

Could she really see him or was this just another facet of her dream, her soul's wish to find the man she'd committed her heart to? Lara descended through the sky to get a better view, puzzled why Dex would be sacked out in a boat with a cell phone tucked under his ear, unless—

Did he plan to search for her?

A visual scan of the vessel showed his GPS device fired up and feeding images of the water. Blankets had been loaded in the back along with a cooler and what looked to be diving equipment. Her heart clenched with emotions she didn't want to deny any longer. He was coming to get her even if he didn't have a clue where to find her. And something about that blind commitment made her realize he believed in the power of psychic connections even if he didn't know how to acknowledge it. He felt as tied to her as she'd grown to him. For her, that meant a telepathic meeting of the minds, but since he didn't view the world through the same lens as her, he wouldn't see it that way. But she knew deep in her gut that they felt the same powerful bond even if Dex wanted to write it off as physical attraction.

Hadn't he admitted to operating blind where she was concerned? Maybe she ought to be giving him more credit for taking risks with her when he didn't even have the safety net of extra senses.

"Dex." Heart filled with tender emotions, she drifted over him the way a body can in astral dreaming.

He responded instantly, sitting up while his cell phone clattered to the floor.

"You're alive." Dex breathed the words on her skin, her body feeling very present in the moment despite the dreamlike nature of her arrival on his boat.

Next to him. On top of him.

God, she hoped she was alive.

"I want to feel you." She straddled his lap where he sat, her knees squeezing his hips. "I feel faint and weak where I've been taken, but being here with you takes that away."

"I can find you." He cupped the base of her skull and stared into her eyes. "Tell me where."

She inched her way down the steely muscles of his thighs, her butt tingling with sweet sensation.

"I don't know where we are. To the east somewhere." She didn't want to waste time on things they couldn't resolve when she could wrap herself around him and take away the cold fear inside her. "I'm scared and I want to feel warm. Hot. Please."

The look in his eyes shifted from one kind of intensity to another. She didn't know how she recognized it, but she experienced the rise of his sexual interest inside her body even before she felt it come to life in his.

He drew her toward him. Focused. Wordless. He pulled her mouth to his and took her lips with open-mouthed greed. His kiss dominated and commanded, freeing her to do nothing but taste him. Submit to the wild, steep pleasure of it.

His hands took control of her hips, seizing them between his open palms. The touch lit up her insides, fanning a flame to bright, billowing proportions. Then he began to rock her, sliding her hips back and forth in a slow ride over his thighs. The motion mimicked sex so thoroughly her juices flowed hot and wet for him.

"Dex." His name was wrenched from her lips, a sharp twinge of longing evident in that lone syllable. "This is real."

It seemed important for him to know that. But whether he thought she meant the sex or the emotions they were feeling, she wasn't sure. The chill of the wind stroked over her and she moved closer to the heat of him.

"Show me." He broke the kiss to issue the dare, his lips wet with the proof of her longing for him. With one hand, he gripped the waistband of her jeans and tugged the fabric right and left in a dance of sweet friction against her sex. "Show me how real it is."

With trembling hands, she reached for the fastenings on her jeans and undid them, opening the fly to a hint of pink panties. He remained perfectly still. Waiting. Watching her through narrowed eyes.

She didn't want to spend the rest of her life proving her claims to him, but because he sat in a motorboat in the middle of a river waiting to find her, this once she would show him what he wanted.

Lifting up on her knees, she hovered above his lap, her hips barely controlling the urge to roll and undulate against him. Instead, she tugged his hand to the patch of pink underwear and guided his fingers into the elastic.

"See?" she whispered, pleasure singing through her at the promise of skin-on-skin contact. "Will you believe me when I'm all around you? When your fingers touch off a current that rocks my whole body?"

Their eyes locked, daring each other on.

"Shouldn't we stop so I can keep searching for you?"

"No." She couldn't stop now if she tried. "Besides the more we connect here, the more likely you'll be able to find me. And if you don't—that is, if you can't—this might be our last time together."

"Never." Dex remained still until Lara rocked her hips back, making more room between her body and the denim. "Do you hear me? That's not going to happen."

He plunged two fingers deep inside her, and she seemed to go boneless from the pleasure, her whole body caving in on him at the slow slide of his sweet touch. He pressed hard, cupping her sex in his hand when he withdrew, and then entering her all over again.

Her jeans slipped farther down her hips, her panties rolling away from his hand as she gave herself over to this teasing abbreviation of sex. The fog on the river lifted, clearing her vision and her purpose as her hips followed the rhythm he set up for her. The sense of freedom and belonging at the same time awed her. She could fly with him, her whole being poised on the precipice of new discovery. Shedding all reservation, she worked herself harder against the counterpressure of his hand. Tension coiled tight between her thighs, and she allowed her hips to grind harder into the pleasure he could bring.

Release broke over her so hard she fell into him, bucking and shaking with the force of her fulfillment. She covered his face with kisses and cries of completion, the bliss so enormous she had to share it.

Without a doubt, the sex was real. It was a connection that buoyed her through the worst moments of her life and brought her—panting and sweating—back to consciousness on a cramped boat in the middle of nowhere.

DEX BOLTED UPRIGHT, confused for a moment, wondering if the phone had rung.

Sweat beaded on his forehead and his back. His skin burned the way it did in those moments before a kick-ass climax. He sat there on his boat, needing to find Lara when she was in danger and what the hell kind of insensitive idiot was he, sporting an erection the size of a Major League bat?

It was a dream.

Yet even as he thought it, he knew it wasn't. Lara had been here. On the boat, peeling her clothes away, asking him to touch her.

For once, he hadn't been insensitive. He'd been clued in, keyed in, and understanding about what she needed. Moreover, he believed she was alive. Firing up the boat, he let his intuition guide him since his phone hadn't actually rung in twenty minutes of waiting to hear back from a friend scanning the river from above with a chopper.

Trusting his gut and a conversation with Lara he once would have written off as a daydream, Dex turned the boat to the east and pushed the accelerator high. Higher.

Full throttle.

Nothing would keep him from finishing what they'd started.

14

LARA HAD ALWAYS BEEN HIRED to find the missing person.

Never before had she *been* the missing person.

And while she'd always experienced a frightening amount of fear and empathy on behalf of the people she helped locate, those dark feelings weren't the same as being bound and gagged in the bottom of a small boat with a mentally unstable man carrying her farther and farther from home.

A massive handgun perched on a pile of olive-green canvas that looked like a small tent. Victor Marek sat on a metal bench seat, his winter coat flapping open in the wind off the water, reminding Lara that she was toe-numbingly cold with no jacket of her own. Although, from the look of the gun resting so close to Marek's hand, she guessed the cold would be the least of her worries.

"Mmf!" she screamed behind her gag, outrage and frustration combining as she pulled herself upright, her hair damp from the water sloshed on the boat floor.

The former football kicker looked at her with dangerously dark eyes, his expression showing none of the uncertainty she remembered from five years ago when he'd waffled for hours on the issue of whether or not he wanted help breaking the alleged curse on his leg.

"No can do, Lara." He continued to row the boat despite the small motor on the back, a fact that surprised her and—she hoped—boded well for Dex catching up to them.

Dex.

Just thinking his name called up a softness inside her, a precious new store of feelings she hadn't taken out and fully examined yet. She knew it would probably be considered unwise to fall for a man over the course of a weekend. But then again, sometimes a woman just *knew.*

Her future was bound up with Dex Brantley's.

Assuming she could free herself enough to talk to Victor Marek, because something told her—not precognition, just good old-fashioned female intuition—that she needed to communicate with her captor if she wanted any hope of escape. She didn't know if she needed to talk him into freeing her or talk to him to slow down their progress, but her instincts shrieked at her to find a way to communicate with him.

"Mmf?" she asked again in a calmer tone, arranging her eyebrows into what she hoped was a politely pleading manner.

Sighing, Victor rested one oar on the boat's edge, letting the cold water drip onto Lara's back as he leaned forward to pry one side of the duct tape from her mouth. The rip of tape from skin had to have broken twenty blood vessels, the sting was so intense it brought tears to her eyes.

"Thank you," she managed, sensing this man had a low threshold for frustration. She wouldn't push him over it. "I'm sorry that Dex Brantley put you in this situation."

Instinct guided her words along with minimal

exposure to police guidelines for dealing with people who'd taken hostages. She minimized eye contact and spoke calmly. Quietly.

"You and me both." He moved again, his hand lifting toward the tape as if to replace it where it had been.

"I just would hate to see the Brantley family curse carried over to you after you've been through so much already." She had no idea what he'd been through, but she gathered he thought himself wronged by Dex.

Vic's hand drooped to his side again, the boat floating idly through the water while Lara tried to keep her teeth from chattering in the cold and dampness.

"Don't you get it? I'm Brantley's curse. I've been dogging him like white on rice for nearly a year. I'm single-handedly running him out of business. And running him out of all three of his houses. Now I'm going to bust up his love life until he's left with nothing. Same way I've got nothing." Vic's tone was flat, his eyes appeared dull and resigned. Unhappy.

Lara debated how hard to push a man clearly on an emotional and mental ledge, but decided it was worth the risk since she guessed he could kill her without a second thought in his present mood.

"There's more to the curse." She tore a bit of her lip on the duct tape since half her mouth remained covered. Blood trickled down onto her gums. "You got the idea for the curse from reading about the old family legend, right? You must know there is a basis for the family's bad luck."

Marek said nothing, his face sullen even as gripped his oars and dipped them both back into the water again.

"I only think it's fair to warn you that hurting Dex while

he is suffering under this bout of bad luck will transfer the curse to you and your family."

His smile was tight.

"My family can't get any worse." Easing up on one oar, he seemed to be steering the boat toward a protected cove on a small island. Lara couldn't see a main building on the land, but there was a decrepit dock and a faded boathouse.

They'd alternated between oar power and the small motor, perhaps in an attempt to stay off the radar of any boats out searching for them. And perhaps they were running out of time to be found if Victor was taking her to this island.

"But still—"

"Look, I've got nothing to lose by robbing Dex of you. He's going to have to experience the unique pain of losing someone he cares about. I hear that's pure hell, and that's what I'm aiming to put him through when he finds out you're chained to this concrete block here at the bottom of the St. Lawrence."

Sneering at her, he rattled the chain attached to a heavy, rough slab.

Cold horror swirled in the pit of her stomach, though she tried not to let him see it.

"The curse is strong, Victor." She addressed him by name and risked a look directly in the eye, needing a read on his emotional state, a hint for how to talk him out of this horrible thing.

What she saw in his lifeless gaze scared her.

"Lucky for me, I'm not going to kill Dexter so I won't inherit any bad shit hanging over his head." Rowing steadily toward the boathouse, Vic didn't even blink as he turned toward her. "It's you who's going to die."

WHERE THE HELL could she be?

Desperation clawed up Dex's spine, scratched along the base of his skull and racked his body with heart-tripping fear. He'd been on the water for an hour with no sign of her. There were almost no boats on the water save a few cargo vessels with loads that needed to be somewhere. But he was looking for his own boat, the watercraft someone had stolen from him. And no small boats had shown up on his radar or within his visual radius.

Who the hell had taken her?

If he could answer that question maybe he would figure out where the shiftless effing rat bastard had taken her.

His cell phone rang while the boat motored east. Reception remained sketchy on the water even though the weather was clearing up. The only places that got solid reception were locations close to big islands or the mainland.

In the last twenty minutes, he'd gotten messages from the park police, state police and the Coast Guard that they were all out looking for Lara by now. Not that he'd run across any of them in his hour of searching.

He thumbed the green button on his cell. "Brantley."

He half hoped to hear Lara's voice on the other end. The caller ID was fogged over with exposure to water.

"Dex, it's Trish. I know you didn't want to be disturbed this weekend, but I wasn't sure if you'd gotten my messages or heard from Massimo."

He so didn't want to hear about work right now. The desperation to find Lara morphed into anger at Trish, at the 24-7 work life he'd created for himself.

"Damn it, Trish, the woman I hired this weekend has been taken hostage and I need to find her. I don't give a shit about Massimo right now." His eyes burned as he stared through the haze over the water, his vision bleary from wanting to see any sign of Lara.

"Have you called the police? Do you need me up there or anyone else from the office? I can be there in two hours if I can help."

Regret stung him for yelling at her. He had a kick-ass staff that had stayed with him through the rampant defection of star-power clients and major upheaval that had kept them all on their toes.

"I really appreciate that, Trish." Something close to tears burned his eyes along with the bleariness. God, he hadn't known jack shit what it felt like to be cursed until Lara's safety, maybe even her life, had been threatened. "I'd rather have you safe in New York, but any prayers you can wing up here would be—" He blinked hard. Took a breath. "That would be great."

He pictured Trish back in his Manhattan office. She was raising three kids in the New Jersey suburbs, commuting every day and showing up with leftovers for him on a regular basis because she spent any free minutes indulging a love of cooking. And with all she juggled, all she managed at home and work, she still put herself on the line to help him out. He needed to give her a raise. Furthermore, he needed to realize how damn lucky he'd been every day of his life before now.

"You've got 'em, Dex. I'll call Massimo personally and tell him he needs to be patient. He ought to know better than to listen to washed-up, bitter former athletes when it comes to—"

"What?" Dex slowed the boat to be sure he heard Trish

properly. Something about her words reminded him of the long list of enemies he'd compiled, a list he'd never narrowed down sufficiently. "What bitter former athletes?"

"Massimo has been trying to tell you all weekend. Victor Marek has been aggressively recommending Massimo doesn't sign with you."

Victor Marek.

The name rolled around in his mind along with his impressions of the kicker over the years. It might be a stretch to believe the guy could be responsible for something like this if he looked at just the facts, but if he went with his gut…well…

That explained a whole hell of a lot. The smashed trophy cases. A saboteur with enough cash and free time to follow Dex all over the country to set houses on fire and cause trouble. Lara had described an angry man in a fight when she'd thought about the person responsible for the rope to Dex's boat being cut.

Maybe she'd been seeing the crush of a tackle on a gridiron, the angry pile of bodies leaping onto one another.

Dex's mind cranked into high gear, the missing pieces and misunderstood connections all of a sudden coming together in a perfect, clear picture. Logic and instinct worked in sync until he realized the conclusion wasn't much of a stretch after all.

Marek had bought a piece of investment property up here a few years ago. Land he'd never developed—land he'd wanted after seeing Dex's home.

"Thank you for telling me, Trish." He steered the boat hard to the right, confident he knew exactly where he was going. And hell, based on the timing of Trish's call with information when he needed it most, he wondered if they weren't all psychically connected somehow.

Jesus H. Christ, he had to find Lara and tell her that.

Minutes stretched out into taut, endless blocks of time as he skimmed the surface of the water, his boat maxed out at the speed equivalent of about sixty-five miles an hour. The hull lifted high out of the water, the spray from the rooster tail wake whipping the back of his jacket anytime he veered left or right.

He'd actually been extremely close to Marek's property, and while he could get there by sight, he looked up the co-ordinates on a navigational map to relay the information to the search parties looking for Lara. They were all heading there now, but he would be the first to arrive, the first to circle the vacant island to search for signs of life.

Hell. The turn of phrase made his gut churn. There *would* be signs of life, damn it. He'd meant it would be up to him to locate Vic and Lara since he'd been closer to her than any professional investigators or rescue workers.

The island appeared suddenly to his right when he curved around a bigger piece of land beside it. There were no homes, no condos here. Just a weathered cedar boat-house and a small dock.

Dex's stolen boats bobbed in the water, anchored about a hundred yards off one side of the dock.

He raced closer, approaching at a reckless speed, but he couldn't be sure how far Vic had gotten with Lara. Were they already on the island? Or could they have simply stopped off here to pick up a different boat, one the search parties would never recognize?

Frustration steamed through him until he overshot the

stolen boat and saw them—two familiar heads in the water, hiding behind the shelter of the bow. Vic's eyes were narrowed in concentration. Lara's eyes remained wide with fear.

A shot rang out before Dex could process what happened, the windshield on his boat shattering.

Dex dived off the deck and into the frigid river. Water filled his heavy jacket and boots, yanking him down deep. He kicked off the footwear and shoved off the coat, trying to keep his bearings and avoid the motor of his boat. Even after his boat sped past, the water remained turbulent, preventing him from seeing where Vic was.

Would Vic shoot Lara or drown her in the time it took Dex to reach them?

Adrenaline must have kept his lungs full of air for longer than he ever thought possible because he swam underwater until his eyes burned and his head was about to explode. Still, he spotted the moorings of the dock and the struggle of two bodies beside the stolen boat.

He had to reach them before anything happened to Lara. She'd been alive a moment ago. He hadn't come all this way only to reach her a second too late.

With no choice but to come up for a breath, Dex broke through the surface as fast as possible, gasping and guzzling air. Lara's screams scared the hell out of him while another shot skimmed across the river.

"Stay away, Brantley!" Vic shouted to him, his voice hoarse with anger or exhaustion or some emotion Dex had never seen from him before. "You're too late."

Only then did Dex realize Lara's screams had stopped.

Through the swirl of hazy fog over the water, he saw Victor holding her beneath the surface.

The moment drew out in slow-motion horror. Dex started to dive back under the water almost immediately, and the visual of Vic's snarl, his arm braced against something beneath the water, burned instantly in his head.

But oddly, another image blasted into Dex's consciousness in those seconds before he disappeared underwater. A woman dressed in some kind of period costume stood on the dock above Victor, her long, ruffled white skirts brushing the weathered wood planks as she pitched rocks at Victor's head.

Dex figured he'd lost too much oxygen and his brain was hallucinating bizarre images. He knifed through the water, his arms cutting a swath through the river to propel him forward to Lara.

If an oxygen-starved man was going to dream up someone coming to his aid, why hadn't he imagined the cops or a machine-gun-toting helicopter? Who the hell pictured a fragile little woman in a turn-of-the-century dress with her hair in a bun?

But then the muddle of his thoughts cleared as he spied Lara underwater.

Lara.

The sight of her sped him faster to her side. He prepared to yank her out of Vic's grasp, but she sank into him easily, as if Victor had released her.

She felt heavy. Fear choked him and he prayed it was unconsciousness that made her drop like a stone into his arms.

Hauling her to the surface, he saw the hull of a U.S.

Coast Guard patrol boat. Two agents stood on deck with their weapons aimed at Victor while another agent hauled Vic out of the water. And while at the back of his mind, Dex registered gratitude for the help, his focus remained on Lara's limp body as he swam toward the shore.

"She needs help!" Dex shouted, his voice hoarse. "Medical help. Now."

Breathless, he pushed them toward the shore on sheer will alone, his body freezing with the cold. Lara's face had gone milky-white, her hair plastered to her skin along with some dirt and weeds.

"Lara." He had no medical training, no earthly clue what to do. And holy hell, he couldn't let her die now. "Lara, honey, don't let me be too late."

His feet raked across the bottom of the muddy sand and he stumbled ashore, their bodies falling onto land in a tangle of sopping clothes. He cradled Lara on the way down, but when her back hit the sand she began to choke.

Gasping, wheezing, coughing up water, she seemed to come to life again in front of his eyes.

Fear poured out of him with every bucket of river water Lara expelled from her lungs. Water dripped down his face and he was pretty sure he cried, but they were both so drenched he couldn't be sure what the hell was happening beyond the fact that she was okay. Safe. Whole.

Thank you, God.

Dex didn't even know what happened with Vic and the Coast Guard as a park police boat pulled up and pried Lara from his arms to take her to the hospital. He just knew the worst hour of his life was over.

No amount of bad luck in the rest of his life could ever compare to what he'd just been through, and from now on, come what may, he was going to remember what a lucky bastard he really was.

15

"I CAN HANDLE the steps on my own."

Lara wrapped her arms around Dex's neck as he carried her up the huge marble staircase toward the master bedroom two days later.

"The hospital said you need to regain strength." He'd made multiple copies of her discharge papers so that his chef, his assistant and anyone else in the house would know what Lara needed to be well.

The chef had returned when he'd heard about Lara's accident and agreed to stay on for a while. And Dex's completely charming, sweetly maternal assistant had shown up even though Dex had told her he had things under control. And although she'd brought him a homemade pie from four hundred miles away, she'd also brought a satellite tech to upgrade the service to Dex's house so Trish could stay in touch with him. Clever woman.

"That was yesterday. The doctor discharged me because I'm fine, remember?"

He took the last few steps, frowning.

"I know, and I was freaking worried to death about you the whole time. Can you just humor me and give me a few days to see for myself that you're okay?"

She smiled, already plotting the sensual ways she could catch him off guard in his vigilant watch over her as he strode through the double doors into the master suite. The place they'd spent that first amazing night together.

Lara looked back over his shoulder toward the stairs and was surprised to see the great-grandfather's mistress standing at the top of the stairs in her long gown and upswept hair. The woman—the spirit—smiled and waved. A blessing from the other side, perhaps? She vanished as fast as she'd appeared, leaving them alone.

Somehow, Lara guessed she wouldn't be seeing the spirit at Brantley House again. The woman may have died unhappy, but she'd found some sort of peace this weekend. Maybe she'd wanted to help a Brantley man see past his own stubbornness to find happiness. Or maybe she had just needed a century to forgive her long-ago lover.

Secretly, Lara suspected the woman had just wanted to share her story with someone who could hear her. Someone who would share her pain. Lara had listened, and sometimes that was enough to heal an old wound.

"You realize coming back into this bedroom is already giving me a few ideas for ways to prove my good health." She turned in his arms, her breasts grazing his chest until he groaned.

"You nearly died." His dark eyes fixed hers with an unwavering stare and she felt the bond between them strengthen and grow.

She had the feeling he sensed that, too.

And while she wasn't sure if she was ready for a relationship that knocked her off her psychic game, she was powerless to walk away from this man.

Especially when he still held her tight even as he laid her down on the massive four-poster bed.

"Thank you for saving me." She'd said it once already to him, in the hospital when she'd been weary with exhaustion and half-conscious most of the day, but she wanted to tell him again now that she could explain how grateful she was.

Victor Marek had been taken into custody by the park police, the jurisdiction being more straightforward for them to prosecute him, apparently. He'd surrendered quietly, admitting to being off medication for an anger disorder that had probably also caused some of his problems as a player. Lara had given her statement from the comfort of her hospital bed, with Dex at her side. The police assured her they had more than enough evidence to convict him on multiple charges including attempted murder, harassment, criminal mischief, and—thanks to a call from the fire marshal's office—two counts of arson.

"I couldn't let him hurt you." He shifted to sit beside her on the fresh white spread someone had put on the bed since she'd been in the house last. "I brought you into this and it was my fault that you became a target. I couldn't— I had no choice but to make sure you were safe."

His words warmed her insides, even as she half wished there had been something else driving his search for her, something more personal.

The sun shone through the French doors across from the bed, bringing a fresh light into the mansion now that— as far as she was concerned—the curse had been broken. She basked in the warmth of the sunshine and Dex's tender concern even as she knew her time at Brantley House was coming to an end.

"You weren't any more at fault than me." She wished he would put his hands on her, but he'd been oh-so-careful with her since he'd pulled her out of the water. "Becoming a missing person this weekend made me realize that I shouldn't feel any shame about taking on smaller cases, because if I get involved in people's problems early on, I might be able to stop some of them from being in that situation in the first place. If I hadn't been psychically blinded by my attraction to you, I would have put the pieces together faster about Victor and saved both of us from a lot of heartache."

"You can't always save people, Lara. I didn't even get you involved until Victor was already determined to take everything from me." He leaned forward to fluff her pillow, putting his cheek within kissable range.

She licked the ridge of his cheekbone, her tongue darting along his clean-shaven face. The scent of after-shave made her legs weak with want. And oh God, how would she ever go back to her carriage house offices in Albany, hundreds of miles from this man after everything they'd shared this weekend?

"But it was still the right choice to help you, even if it wasn't the kind of job that makes headlines for its community service value, you know?" She was already penning her response to her mother's friends in her mind, determined to find a way for psychics to shatter old stereotypes about their work and serve a larger segment of people who needed their help. "Sometimes people sense negative energy in their lives long before they encounter any actual danger and we shouldn't be afraid to get involved with those smaller cases to prevent them from spiraling into bigger dangers."

She felt a new contentment with her work, having been held at gunpoint. Victor Marek had planned to tie a concrete block to her ankle and send her to the bottom of the river. Facing death had made so many other worries in her life feel petty and out of place.

Dexter brushed her hair away from her face, his warm fingers stroking her temples.

"I've been thinking a lot about your work the last couple of days." He appeared distinctly uncomfortable and she supposed this would be the time when he'd tell her that he couldn't get past the sideshow connotations of her job.

Although she wouldn't remain involved with someone who didn't respect her career, she could at least give him the benefit of some publicity from her visit. Now that she no longer cared about maintaining some artificial wall of respectability between her and the world, what did it matter if she advertised her presence on Brantley Island?

"You know, now that I've come to a new peace with the kinds of jobs I'm going to take, I would be glad to go to your local paper and tell them all about my visit and how the curse has ended."

She didn't know if Dex was ready to hear how the curse had ended, but she'd be willing to believe the newspaper writer would love it.

"Honestly?" His lips lifted in a half grin as he stroked the long angora hairs along the neckline of her purple sweater. "That's kind of you, but I've decided nothing that bad happened in my life until Victor took you. Everything else leading up to that seemed incredibly fixable by comparison."

"Still, it might be good for your career—"

"Lara?" He stopped picking at her sweater, his expression serious again. "I had a moment when I was in the water—when Victor was holding you under. I thought I saw something on the dock behind him. A woman—"

Everything inside her stilled.

"Who?" She would feign ignorance, unwilling to lead him with any visions of her own. "Do you know who it was?"

His brow furrowed and he shook his head as if he didn't believe it himself.

"I thought maybe she was some local reenactor or something because she was dressed in the kinds of clothes that were popular around the islands when this was still a social hot spot. Sort of like the dresses on the women in those paintings on the walls of the guest suite."

Excitement built, bubbling up her chest although she tried to swallow it down.

"You saw a woman dressed in a turn-of-the-century gown. Young or old? What was she doing?"

"Aren't you surprised?" He studied her, perhaps guessing she knew more than she was saying. "Don't you think it's weird I saw a young woman in a crazy outfit pitching rocks at Vic's head while he held you under? Or do you think our hallucinations mean something significant?"

"It depends. Did you have any other interesting hallucinations while I was held hostage?" She sat up on the bed, unwilling to play the passive patient for him anymore when she was on the verge of a major breakthrough.

"I had a dream—" He stopped abruptly. "What are you doing?"

She got up off the bed and walked across the room toward the bag of her clothes and personal belongings from the hospital. Dex's assistant had claimed her wet things from the E.R. and had everything laundered before they came home. She was already enjoying the thrill of the surprise she was about to dish up for him.

"What kind of dream?" She found what she wanted to show him, knowing there was a small chance she might freak him out for good and send him running. But she understood she had to take the chance if they wanted any shot at a relationship down the road.

"It's kind of—embarrassing, I guess. I had a totally hot dream about you in these hot-pink panties during a twenty-minute power nap before I knew where to go—"

She threw the item across the room and watched his athlete's reflexes react automatically. He snatched her pink thong out of the air and stared down at it.

His jaw literally fell away from the rest of his mouth.

"Oh my God."

"You saved me then, too, Dex. Vic sort of choked the air out of me when he first found me and I went unconscious in that floating state where I could have gone either way." Life or death. Dex or a more peaceful world. Her choice had been simple. Clear-cut. "I came to you when you were dreaming."

His jaw snapped shut, his fingers toying with the fabric as if he remembered exactly how the underwear had figured into their lovemaking.

"Who the hell was the woman I saw on the dock throwing rocks?"

"Your great-grandfather's mistress." Lara would lay it all on the line and if Dex thought she was crazy, she would know this wasn't meant to be. But oh God, her heart ached for him to see beyond the surface, to see with his other senses.

"You—can't be serious."

Her heart stopped in her chest and she held her breath. Waiting.

"I'm very serious." *Please believe me.* "She appeared on that deserted island right when I needed her most. I think her spirit has been close to us all weekend, as if she wanted to see what happened between us. Maybe she will rest easy now that she's seen you're not like her long-ago lover. She knows I'm safe with you."

"I still think that long-ago night on the staircase was just a tragic accident. I've been thinking about that ever since you saw their fight that morning. But maybe we'll never know for sure." He seemed troubled about that fact, but she didn't know how to reassure him.

Some mysteries were best left in the past.

"I saw her on the dock, Lara." He seemed to need for her to believe him. "With my eyes."

"You saw her, all right." She didn't tell him his eyes had nothing to do with it.

It was enough for her that he'd admitted having a vision some people would have dismissed as completely fanciful.

Walking back to the bed, Lara stood beside it. Waiting. Once she lay down in the same room with Dex again, she didn't know if she'd be able to walk away.

"The sex while we were dreaming—" His gaze went a little starry-eyed and she liked knowing that time together had been damn transporting for him, too.

"The chemistry between us definitely hasn't been a problem." She could easily sign on for a lifetime of hotter-than-hot nights with Dex in her bed.

"Move in with me."

Dex loosened his tie, as if settling in for a difficult job.

"What?" She blinked dumbly, not expecting that kind of statement from him.

"Move up here with me. Full-time, part-time, on a temporary basis, I don't know. Whatever you're ready for." He moved around to the other side of the bed, closer to her. "Don't you want to see where this leads if we spend some time together?"

He was serious.

Lara stared at him in his gold cuff links and pressed shirt, wondering if she could withstand a full-court press from a man reputed to be one of the most persuasive in his business. At least, that's what Victor had told her before he'd pushed her over the side of the boat. He'd said it was a pity such an unscrupulous man could have been born with so much persuasive talent to attract up-and-coming athletes.

Lara figured it was more likely people were attracted to Dex because he possessed the easy confidence of a man who could get things done. She'd seen for herself that was true.

And she knew without a doubt the part about Dex being unscrupulous had never been the case. He'd already received half a dozen phone calls from former clients who were flailing without him and who regretted ever leaving his representation.

"I don't know, Dex." She thought about the carriage house she just painted. Her assistant, Jamie, counted on his part-time job with her to help him pay for college. "I just moved into a new space, but more importantly…"

She didn't know how to admit the things that scared her most.

"What?" He braced her shoulders, one hand on each, subtly demanding she confront this. Him. "Tell me what it is and we'll fix it."

She imagined he would try, too. How many times had he led successful negotiations to make all parties happy in his line of work?

"I don't want to mess up your career because of your association with me, but I also don't want to hide what I do." She wouldn't keep her tea leaf reading or past life regression work in the closet. "But I also can't afford to downplay some of the more unorthodox things I do. I like ghost hunting in my free time, for crying out loud. How's that going to help your image as Joe Sophisticated Agent?"

"Sophisticated?" He squeezed her shoulders and backed her temptingly close to his bed. "Hell, Lara. I'm wearing a tie with an NBA logo and the jersey number of one of my clients. I've got a trophy room that amounts to the biggest freaking sports paraphernalia collection on the East Coast. I invite guys up here to play pool and PlayStation into the late hours because that stuff's fun for me. No one is going to bat an eye if I have a hot psychic living with me. You'll probably have to fight off requests to guess outcomes of big league games."

"Dex, you're a megamillionaire with a French chef and three homes, even if two are burned down. There's a little bit of a lifestyle disconnect—"

"The chef is French Canadian, sweetheart—he's very touchy about the difference." He pushed her back down to the bed, his face full of tender concern that soothed some of her worries. "As for the three properties, I think I'd like to take the insurance money and pour it into making this place something special to prove to the world that Brantley House is curse free. I might even give in and open it to the public a few days a week for some extra cash. You could reopen your business in the carriage house here. Hell, I'll convert a whole barn if you like. You can give readings to the tourists who come to snap photos of the house."

"I could give a ghost tour." She said it before she even processed the wisdom of it, but thankfully he seemed to like the idea by the way he threw his head back and laughed.

"Now that's priceless. The historical society would love it." He lowered one hand to her knee and massaged lightly. "And I'd love having you here. Day and night."

The gentle massage of her knee moved higher up her thigh, and while she refused to become a hostage of her own desires, she also wouldn't ignore an incredibly enticing element of their relationship.

If not for the amazing, crawl-out-of-her-skin attraction to Dex, she would have never discovered what an intriguing, strong man lay beneath his slick surface.

And wasn't it interesting how even an accomplished psychic could use the occasional lesson in seeing without using her eyes?

"I'd have to offer to relocate a part-time employee." She wouldn't renege on something Jamie counted on. "A guy."

"As long as you're sleeping with me, I don't care how many guys you invite." He frowned. "For that matter, I invite athletes to this house all the time for wine-and-dine weekends. I'm going to have to beat the men off with a stick."

"Does that present a problem?" She couldn't believe she was actually considering running blind into a relationship where she couldn't use her psychic senses in regard to her partner.

"Hell no. I already sent one guy to jail for touching you. I'll just make sure to announce that early and often when male guests come to stay." He wound one hand around the back of her neck while his other trekked up her thigh. "Now does that mean you're saying yes?"

All her senses tingled as if conspiring to make her agree. Then again, the tingling might have been related to the wicked things Dex was doing with his fingers as he slid them up her thigh and beneath her skirt.

"Yes. I'll at least give it a try and see, but you have to promise me if it starts not working, you won't hesitate to tell me because I'll be powerless to read your mind."

"Thank you." He pushed her down to the bed and stroked the soft skin of her inner thigh until she wriggled with want. "Thank you for saying yes. And you won't ever have to wonder how I'm feeling because I'll be showing you every single night you sleep under my roof."

His hand crept higher. Higher.

"Dex." She wanted him to cover her, to celebrate the happiest decision she'd ever made.

"I know that dream was real on some level that day on the water." He tugged the neck of her sweater down and kissed the top of one breast. "But since I'm still an old-fashioned, reality-based kind of guy, do you think we can relive it right now?"

"Reality definitely has its place," she murmured, caught up in the seductive spell only he could weave around her.

"You saved me, too, you know." The motion of his hand stopped on her leg and she forced her eyes open. "You showed me what's important to me just by being you."

Another piece of her heart melted away and floated toward him. At this rate she would be well and truly in love with the man before she moved a single suitcase into her palatial new home.

"I—" She didn't know what to say. She just wanted to wrap herself around him and never let go. "I'm glad."

"And you don't need to be worried about a psychic blind spot where I'm concerned." He lay down next to her, his strong, lean body tantalizing hers with the graze of hard muscle.

"I don't?" She would have bought into anything he said at that moment, her legs turning to jelly at his touch.

"No." He bent to kiss the hollow under her ear, then breathe on the spot that he'd left wet and vulnerable. "Because you may think you can't read me from a psychic perspective, but you can obviously connect with me on a sexual psychic level since we shared that dream time together."

She stilled, eyes flying open this time.

"That's right." She shivered in pleasant anticipation. "You might really be onto something there."

Maybe she could read him in some ways, and maybe they could expand their connections to new levels.

"Soon I'll be able to just think about making you orgasm and two rooms away your thighs will clench suddenly in the middle of taking a shower or while you're talking to your clients."

"You wicked, wicked man." She arched up into him, hot and ready for his kisses.

And whatever other enchanted pleasures their shared future might bring.

* * * * *

Don't miss Joanne Rock's next book,
UP CLOSE AND PERSONAL!
Coming in May 2008 from Harlequin Blaze.

Enjoy a sneak preview of
MATCHMAKING WITH A MISSION
by B.J. Daniels,
part of the WHITEHORSE, MONTANA *miniseries.*
Available from Harlequin Intrigue
in April 2008.

Nate Dempsey has returned to Whitehorse to uncover the truth about his past…

Nate sensed someone watching the house and looked out in surprise to see a woman astride a paint horse just on the other side of the fence. He quickly stepped back from the filthy second-floor window, although he doubted she could have seen him. Only a little of the June sun pierced the dirty glass to glow on the dust-coated floor at his feet as he waited a few heartbeats before he looked out again.

The place was so isolated he hadn't expected to see another soul. Like the front yard, the dirt road was waist-high with weeds. When he'd broken the lock on the back door, he'd had to kick aside a pile of rotten leaves that had blown in from last fall.

As he sneaked a look, he saw that she was still there, staring at the house in a way that unnerved him. He shielded his eyes from the glare of the sun off the dirty window and studied her, taking in her head of long blond hair that feathered out in the breeze from under her Western straw hat.

She wore a tan canvas jacket, jeans and boots. But it was the way she sat astride the brown-and-white horse that nudged the memory.

He felt a chill as he realized he'd seen her before. In that very spot. She'd been just a kid then. A kid on a pretty paint horse. Not this one—the markings were different. Anyway, it couldn't have been the same horse, considering the last time he had seen her was more than twenty years ago. That horse would be dead by now.

His mind argued it probably wasn't even the same girl. But he knew better. It was the way she sat the horse, so at home in a saddle and secure in her world on the other side of that fence.

To the boy he'd been, she and her horse had represented freedom, a freedom he'd known he would never have—even after he escaped this house.

Nate saw her shift in the saddle, and for a moment he feared she planned to dismount and come toward the house. With Ellis Harper in his grave, there would be little to keep her away.

To his relief, she reined her horse around and rode back the way she'd come.

As he watched her ride away, he thought about the way she'd stared at the house—today and years ago. While the smartest thing she could do was to stay clear of this house, he had a feeling she'd be back.

Finding out her name should prove easy, since he figured she must live close by. As for her interest in Harper House... He would just have to make sure it didn't become a problem.

* * * * *

Be sure to look for
MATCHMAKING WITH A MISSION
and other suspenseful Harlequin Intrigue stories,
available in April
wherever books are sold.

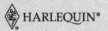

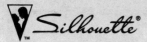

n o c t u r n e™

The Bloodrunners
trilogy continues with book #2.

The hunt meant more to Jeremy Burns than dominance—
it meant facing the woman he left behind. Once
Jillian Murphy had belonged to Jeremy, but now she was
the Spirit Walker to the Silvercrest wolves. It would take
more than the rights of nature for Jeremy to renew his
claim on her—and she would not go easily once he had.

LAST WOLF
HUNTING

by RHYANNON BYRD

Available in April wherever books are sold.

Be sure to watch out for the last book,
Last Wolf Watching, available in May.

SN61785

HARLEQUIN®
Super Romance®

Celebrate the joys of motherhood!
In this collection of touching stories,
three women embrace their maternal
instincts in ways they hadn't expected.
And even more surprising is how true
love finds them.

Mothers of the Year

With stories by
Lori Handeland
Rebecca Winters
Anna DeStefano

Look for Mothers of the Year,
available in April
wherever books are sold.

REQUEST YOUR FREE BOOKS!

2 FREE NOVELS PLUS 2 FREE GIFTS!

HARLEQUIN®

Blaze™

Red-hot reads!

HB08

introduces...

Lust in Translation
A sexy new international miniseries.

Don't miss the first book...

FRENCH KISSING
by **Nancy Warren**

April 2008

N.Y. fashionista Kimi Renton knows sexy
photographer Holden McGregor is a
walking fashion disaster. And she's tried
to make him over. But when they're
lip-locked, it's ooh-la-la all the way!

LUST IN TRANSLATION
Because sex is the same
in any language!

COMING NEXT MONTH

#387 ONE FOR THE ROAD Crystal Green
Forbidden Fantasies

A cross-country trek. A reckless sexual encounter. Months ago, Lucy Christie wouldn't have considered either one a possibility. But now she is on the road, looking for thrills, adventure...sex. And the hot cowboy Lucy meets on the way seems just the man for the job....

#388 SEX, STRAIGHT UP Kathleen O'Reilly
Those Sexy O'Sullivans, Bk. 2

It's all on the line when Catherine Montefiore's family legacy is hit by a very public scandal. In private, she's hoping hot Irish hunk Daniel O'Sullivan can save the day. He's got all the necessary skills and, straight up or not, Catherine will have a long drink of Daniel any way she can get him....

#389 FRENCH KISSING Nancy Warren
Lust in Translation

New York fashionista Kimi Renton *knows* sexy photographer Holden McGregor is a walking fashion disaster. And she's tried to make him over. But when they're lip-locked it's *ooh la-la* all the way!

#390 DROP DEAD GORGEOUS Kimberly Raye
Love at First Bite, Bk. 2

Dillon Cash used to be the biggest geek in Skull Creek, Texas—until a vampire encounter changed him into a lean, mean sex machine. Now every woman in town wants a piece of the hunky cowboy. Every woman, that is, except his best friend, Meg Sweeney. But he'll convince her....

#391 NO STOPPING NOW Dawn Atkins

A gig as cameraperson on Doctor Nite's cable show is a coup for Jillian James and her documentary on bad-for-you bachelors. But behind the scenes, Brody Donegan is sexier than she expected. How can she get her footage if she can't keep out of his bed?

#392 PUTTING IT TO THE TEST Lori Borrill
Blush

Matt Jacobs is the man to beat—and Carly Abrams is determined to do what it takes to outsmart him on a matchmaking survey—even cheat. But Carly's problems don't *really* start until Matt—the star of her nighttime fantasies—wants to put her answers to the test!

HBCNM0308